IS THE SADDLE CLUB BREAKING UP?

"What's the matter, Lisa?" Estelle, a new rider at the stables, asked.

"I'm looking for Stevie and Carole," Lisa explained. "We were supposed to meet here. I'm sure they left Pine Hollow by the time I did, so where are they?"

"Carole Hanson and Stevie Lake?" Estelle asked. Lisa nodded. "But I saw them go—Carole went off in the truck with the woman doctor, and Stevie saddled up her pony, Nickel, and was taking him out into the field."

Lisa got a deep sinking feeling. It was clear that both Carole and Stevie had forgotten The Saddle Club meeting they were supposed to have. Each was so wrapped up in her own special project that she didn't even remember *Lisa's* special project! Lisa was just about to explode with anger and hurt. How could her best friends let her down?

ALL THE LIVING
by Claudia Mills

THE BRONZE KING
by Suzy McKee Charnas

THE GHOST IN THE THIRD ROW
by Bruce Coville

THE GHOST WORE GRAY
by Bruce Coville

THE GREAT MOM SWAP
by Betsy Haynes

HORSE CRAZY (The Saddle Club, Book #1)
by Bonnie Bryant

HORSE SHY (The Saddle Club, Book #2)
by Bonnie Bryant

A HORSE OF HER OWN
by Joanna Campbell

JANET HAMM NEEDS A DATE FOR THE DANCE
by Eve Bunting

THE KIDNAPPING OF COURTNEY VAN ALLEN
& WHAT'S-HER-NAME by Joyce Cool

LIZARD MUSIC
by D. Manus Pinkwater

RIDING HOME
by Pamela Dryden

TAFFY SINCLAIR AND THE MELANIE
MAKE-OVER by Betsy Haynes

TAFFY SINCLAIR AND THE ROMANCE
MACHINE DISASTER by Betsy Haynes

A WHOLE SUMMER OF WEIRD SUSAN
by Louise Ladd

THE SADDLE CLUB

HORSE SENSE

BONNIE BRYANT

A BANTAM SKYLARK BOOK®
NEW YORK · TORONTO · LONDON · SYDNEY · AUCKLAND

RL 5, 009-012

HORSE SENSE

A Bantam Skylark Book/February 1989

—for Neil

1

"I CAN TELL I'm really getting better at riding," Lisa Atwood announced to her two best friends with a smile. "Max is only giving me four instructions at a time now—instead of the *eight* he gave me during my first few lessons!"

Carole Hanson and Stevie Lake laughed along with Lisa. Max Regnery, their riding teacher at Pine Hollow Stables, was quite a character sometimes. But they also understood the complexity of riding well. There were always dozens of things to remember at once!

The girls were lounging contentedly in Stevie's room, talking about their favorite subject: horses. The three friends were the members of The Saddle Club, and this get-together was a "meeting." The girls had created the Club, with only two requirements: The members had to be horse crazy and they had to be willing to help one another when help was needed. At the moment, with no problems or crises in evidence, the girls were lazily talking about riding.

Lisa sat cross-legged on Stevie's bed. She twirled her long light brown hair around one finger as she and her friends talked. Lisa was petite and fine-boned, and she looked younger than her thirteen years. Also, the clothes her mother steered her into choosing—classic styles, like pleated plaid skirts and penny loafers—exaggerated her good-little-girl look. Occasionally Lisa daydreamed about having her hair cut in spikes or buying some offbeat clothes at the secondhand store at the mall, but there wasn't enough rebel in her to defy her mother—or, usually, anybody else.

Although a year older than her friends, Lisa was the newest rider of the group. She'd only begun a few months before. She'd started lessons because her mother thought every well-brought-up young girl should know how to ride ("—and dance and paint and play the piano and do needlework, and every other boring thing you could imagine!" Lisa had said in exasperation one day). Then, Lisa had surprised her mother by becoming very interested in riding—and had especially surprised herself, and even Max, by how good she had become at it.

"Well, what were the four instructions?" Stevie asked Lisa with a grin. Stevie was lying on the floor of her room, with her legs propped up on her bed, and her dark blond hair spread out dramatically on the floor. Her hazel eyes were full of mischief. Stevie lived in a comfortable, spacious home with her three brothers (Michael, eight; Alex, her twin; and Chad, fourteen) and her parents. In contrast to Lisa's stylish outfits, Stevie's usually looked like hand-me-downs. She rode in jeans and beat-up cowboy boots. Now, relaxing after riding class, she was lounging in an oversize sweatshirt and a pair of tights.

Stevie was the only rider in her family. Sometimes it was hard for her parents to understand her love of horses, but her commitment had finally convinced them Stevie was serious about riding—perhaps because it was the only thing she *was* serious about. Stevie was a practical joker and frequently in trouble. Somehow, though, Stevie always managed to come out on top. To Lisa, that was one of Stevie's most endearing qualities.

Lisa had to think for a moment to remember Max's instructions. She rolled her eyes and said in a deep, serious voice, "'Heels down, toes in, look straight ahead, and'—" she paused, laughing, then resumed sternly, "and, 'stop talking to your horse!'"

Her friends joined Lisa in a burst of laughter. Max not only taught riding but also owned Pine Hollow Stables. And he was famous for certain idiosyncrasies, among them his belief that horses couldn't understand English. He told his riders that a horse would appreciate the sound of a reassuring word now and again, but they were never to speak *instructions* such as "whoa." For instructions, the rider should always use "aids"— signals with hands, legs, and a riding crop.

"What were you saying to Pepper?" Carole asked.

"I just told him that he should stop looking at the clock—there was another half hour to go in class!"

"You're right, you know. When Pepper decides class should be over, he gets very 'barny,' doesn't he?" Any horse in a hurry to get back to his stall was called barny.

Carole was the most experienced rider of the three girls, having ridden all her life on the Marine Corps bases where her father, now a colonel, had been stationed. Lisa thought Carole was beautiful, with her wavy black hair that hung loose to her shoulders and her intense big brown eyes. Lisa knew that Carole dreamed of owning a stable one day. She wanted to breed horses, train them, and, most of all, to ride them. Riding was the most important thing in her life. So Lisa was always pleased when Carole agreed with her observations about horses.

"He sure does," Lisa said. "Every time we passed the door to the stalls, he slowed down and looked that way—just to remind me that we *could* go in there instead of around in circles."

"I rode a horse on the base at Twenty-Nine Palms once," Carole began, "who was so barny that if you took him out, you always had to keep him turned away from the barn. Once he was turned toward home, no matter how far away he was, nothing could keep him from heading back. They nicknamed him Pidge because he was like a homing pigeon!"

4

The girls were laughing when there was a knock at Stevie's door. "It's me, Chad," Stevie's older brother said. He opened the door. "Mom said to tell you that there are cookies in the kitchen if you're hungry. I could bring them up, if you'd like." With that, he disappeared from the door.

"What's that all about?" Carole asked.

"Beats me," Stevie said. "The last time he offered to do anything for me, it was to eat all my Halloween candy when I was six. Tried to convince me I'd get a stomachache. But he volunteered to take the risk himself!"

"I guess brothers can be weird," Carole remarked. "And speaking of weird, did you hear that new French girl shouting at Nero? She was *really* angry. You're taking French, Stevie, could you understand her?"

"I think the words Estelle used *aren't* included in the vocabulary lists that Mlle. Lebrun gives us." She shook her head and grinned wickedly.

"You shouldn't make fun of her," said Lisa, who always tried to be fair. "After all, Estelle is new to this country. I'm sure they just do things differently in France. And it can't be easy to move your entire life to a new country, you know, just because your father's job is here."

"Well, if they do things differently in France, they do them *very* differently," Carole said, almost smirking.

Before Lisa had a chance to ask Carole what she meant, there was another knock at the door. Chad was back with a snack for the girls. He brought a tray with a little plate of cookies and a glass of milk for each of them. By the time he'd finished serving them, the girls had forgotten about Estelle and had started talking about horses again.

"How's Delilah?" Stevie asked Carole. Delilah, a mare at Pine Hollow, was due to deliver a foal within the next month. The foal had been sired by Cobalt, a Thoroughbred who'd had to be put to sleep after his leg had been shattered beyond repair in a jumping accident. After the tragedy of his sudden death, Carole had wanted to give up riding. He'd been her favorite horse to ride, ever. Then she'd learned about Cobalt's foal.

"The vet says she's doing just fine." Carole's eyes lit up with excitement. "In fact, she was examining Delilah today. It's not going to be long now before Delilah delivers, and the vet promises she'll call me when the time comes. I'm so excited!"

"Wouldn't it be great if we could *all* be there?" Lisa said.

"It would probably upset Delilah," Carole said, deflating Lisa. Lisa hoped Carole didn't think that her special love for Cobalt made her the only one who could help at the foaling. Lisa and Stevie exchanged glances. Carole was very knowledgeable about horses, but there were times when she seemed maybe just a little bit *too* knowledgeable—and a bit too possessive about her knowledge.

"You know what I like best about summer?" Stevie said, changing the subject. Then, without waiting for an answer, she continued. "I like being able to ride every day."

Carole and Lisa nodded. School had let out a few weeks earlier. Now the girls were attending the stable's camp program, which ran every weekday at the stable. Then, if they wanted to, they could ride on weekends as well.

"It's like there's finally enough time to do all the riding I want," Stevie said. "And, not only do we have the foal to look forward to, but I have the feeling there's something else coming up, too."

"What's that?" Lisa asked, suddenly interested.

"Well, I'm not exactly sure, but Max said he wanted to talk to me after camp tomorrow. He sounded *very* mysterious," Stevie finished in her dramatic way.

"The last time Max wanted to talk to you it was because you were getting a C-minus in math, wasn't it?" Carole teased.

"Don't remind me," Stevie said, throwing a pillow at her.

It was a firm rule at Pine Hollow that riding came second to schoolwork. No student was allowed to ride unless school grades were satisfactory. And Max kept a sharp eye on enforcement. "But I ended the year with a B-plus—thanks to Lisa's help—and I'm not at summer school, so it can't have anything to do with that."

"Think he might have found out it was you who put the toad in Veronica's riding hat?" Carole asked.

"No way!" Stevie giggled. "Even though Veronica wanted the toad checked for fingerprints!"

"Boy, I loved the look of horror on her too-perfect face, didn't you?" Carol asked.

Veronica diAngelo was a snooty girl who was in their class at Pine Hollow. Cobalt had belonged to her, and the accident that had cost him his life had been her fault. Even though she was now trying to learn more about riding, she was still Veronica, and the girls didn't like her much.

"You know, I was thinking about trying the toad trick on Estelle, too. After all, one of Pine Hollow's traditions is playing practical jokes on new students," Stevie said.

Practical jokes were Lisa's least-favorite tradition at Pine Hollow. She was about to suggest that it wouldn't be a good idea, when Stevie discarded the notion herself.

"Nah, I don't think so. It might make Max angry and if he gets really mad then he won't tell me what it is he wants to tell me—unless, of course, he's already mad. Then a trick would make it worse. What do you think, Carole?"

"I think it's going to be a colt. . . ." Carole said dreamily.

"Huh? What's that got to do with Max?" Stevie asked.

"Oh, sorry—I was just thinking about Delilah some more."

Lisa watched as Carole and Stevie tried to carry on a conversation, but it was weird because they were talking about different things. Lisa felt a little left out of it. While they were talking back and forth, she began to think about The Saddle Club. She always had fun with Carole and Stevie, but she couldn't help wishing that their club were more official, with rules and regulations. If their meetings were more organized, then they'd all talk about the same subject. That was really the way clubs were supposed to work. Meetings were supposed to be orderly. There was supposed to be new business and old business, election of officers, budgets and motions. Lisa's mother belonged to lots of clubs. That was how it always was. Just because they *called* it The Saddle Club didn't make it a club.

To be a real club, they'd need a constitution. And who, she asked herself, suddenly inspired, was better prepared to make a constitution than the person who had gotten an A on her paper about the United States Constitution? Now Lisa was excited. She had a project too, just like Carole had Delilah and her foal, and Stevie had her mysterious meeting with Max. Lisa grinned to herself, thinking how pleased her friends would be when they found that they belonged to a *real* club.

"Stevie! It's almost time for dinner!" Mrs. Lake's voice came up the stairs. "Lisa? Carole? Isn't it time for your dinner too?" she called out.

"We'd better go," Carole said, taking the hint and tugging her riding jacket out of the soft chair where she'd been sitting. "You know, even though we can ride every day now, there are still two things there's never enough time for."

"Yeah, I know," Stevie said. "Horses and horses, right?"

"Right." Carole nodded. "Riding them and talking about them."

"Make that three things, then," Lisa said grumpily. "We never seem to have enough time for The Saddle Club, either. Or maybe it's just that we don't always use our time right."

"Could be," Carole said agreeably. She and Lisa said their good-byes to Stevie, and then Lisa trailed Carole down the stairs and out the door of Stevie's house.

Lisa was so lost in thought about the articles of the club's unwritten constitution that she barely remembered to say good-bye to Carole when they got to her bus stop.

THE FOLLOWING AFTERNOON, which was a Friday, Stevie headed for Max's office, more than a little bit nervous. Sometimes Max was hard to predict. She *hoped* this meeting was going to be good news, but she wasn't at all sure. Stevie thought she'd seen Max grinning to himself when Veronica discovered the toad in her riding hat, but then again, maybe that wasn't a grin. With Max, it was hard to tell.

And, two days ago, she'd been talking with Lisa during class. Max was more likely to be upset about that; no talking in class was another one of his firm rules. He usually didn't care what happened after class, as long as it didn't hurt the horses. Toads were after class; talking was *in* class.

Just to be on the safe side, Stevie detoured past the good-luck horseshoe. It was nailed next to the mounting area. It was a Pine Hollow tradition that all the riders were supposed to touch the shoe before every ride. The horseshoe had been there as long as anybody could remember, and no rider had ever been seriously hurt at Pine Hollow. Stevie brushed it with her hand on her way to Max's office. It was worn smooth with wishes. Maybe it wouldn't make any difference, she thought, but it made her feel better.

A few seconds later, Max was telling her to come in and sit down. That was when Stevie knew it was all right. One thing that was absolutely predictable about Max was that if he was going to chew you out (and Stevie had plenty of experience at that), he never asked you to sit down. She made herself comfortable in the chair that faced his desk.

"Stevie, do you know what a gymkhana is?" Max asked her.

"Well, sure I do," she told him. "It's a kind of horse show for young riders, only with games and races and things like that—right?"

"Right. In another six weeks, there's going to be a three-day event here for the stable's adult riders and other local competitors. I've been spending so much time planning the other events that I've almost forgotten about my young riders. You'll all have a good time watching the events, but I want to have something special for you as well. And I don't have one extra minute to plan it." He sat forward in his chair and looked Stevie square in the eye. "It has come to my attention that you have a certain knack for funny activities pertaining to horses, not that I approve of a lot of what you've done—we won't even talk about the recent insult to the local toad population—" Stevie giggled involuntarily. Max continued. "—but I'd like to make use of your weird sense of humor. How about it? Can you make up some events for the riders in your class, as well as the really young kids? They should be safe, of course, but fun. And they should require the use of real riding skills. Other than that, it's up to you. Can you do it?"

Could she? "You *bet* I can!" Stevie told him. This was the chance of a lifetime. Her imagination was already in high gear. "You mean things like races and games? Stuff like that?"

"Yes, and they need to be races that can be run by teams of mixed ages—you know, everybody from the six-year-olds on through fifteen. All the older riders will be involved in the three-day event. The gymkhana will take place each afternoon of the three-day event. Mrs. Reg will help you compose the teams. One of the stableboys, probably Red O'Malley, will do the setups for you and will be in charge of getting props. This is a big job, Stevie. If you need help, you can get it—from everybody but me. The success of the gymkhana will pretty much be your responsibility. Are you still game?"

"Am I ever!" she said. "But—"

"Yes?" he asked.

"Well, why *me?*" she asked.

"You're a good rider, Stevie, a really good rider. I'd like to see you take on more responsibility here at Pine Hollow. This seemed like a perfect opportunity. Besides, I really need the help. Look, we'll discuss your ideas every now and again to see where you are. In the meantime—uh-oh, I've got to remember to call Mrs.—uh . . . about the, uh . . ." Max grabbed for the phone. As soon as he'd dialed a number, he began making notes, and it was as if Stevie weren't there anymore. She decided that meant that Max was probably through with her. Quietly, so as not to disturb his concentration, she crept out of his office. He didn't seem to notice.

A gymkhana would be lots of fun and being in charge of it would be even better. She'd read about them and she had heard about one from a cousin of hers who lived in New Jersey, but she'd never actually seen one. She'd need some information about what sort of games they should have, and when it came to getting information at Pine Hollow, no one was more helpful than Mrs. Reg, Max's mother. When his father had died, Max had taken over the stable, and his mother had remained in charge of the tack room and the equipment. She was always full of great horse stories. The only drawback to getting advice from Mrs. Reg was that you had to do something in return—like clean tack.

Like the other Saddle Club members, Stevie loved to ride horses, but knew that horses were at least as much work as pleasure. For every hour spent riding horses, owners probably spent two taking care of them. Another Pine Hollow tradition—and ironclad rule— was that all the riders had to do chores around the stable. Some jobs were officially assigned and others were done as needed; all the riders were simply expected to pitch in. Carole loved horses so much that she'd do anything for them. But Stevie was not thrilled with the messy stable chores. Cleaning tack qualified as a messy stable chore in Stevie's book.

Stevie stepped into the tack room. There, along one wall, was an endless sea of saddles and bridles. One bridle hung above each saddle, adjusted for a specific horse. The first set of tack on the right-hand wall had been assigned to the first horse in the right-hand stable. Since they were cleaned methodically, there was always a marker by the next set of tack due for a saddle soaping. Stevie automatically picked up the tack and the soap can and sponge, shooing away the kitten that had pounced on the bridle she carried, and walked into Mrs. Reg's office. She sat down on the tack box near Mrs. Reg's desk and began her work.

"What can I do for you, child?" Mrs. Reg asked. She knew Stevie wouldn't submit to saddle soaping un-asked unless she needed something.

"What do you know about gymkhanas?" Stevie asked.

Mrs. Reg smiled broadly. "Oh, I think we can cook something up, don't you?" she asked.

Stevie filled her sponge with saddle soap and began cleaning the saddle's flaps while she listened.

"WE'RE LOOKING FOR definite signs now," the vet, Judy Barker, told Carole. The two of them stood outside the foaling stall where Delilah was being kept until her foal was born. The foaling stall was different from the other horses' stalls; it was larger and specially designed to be completely safe for a foal. There were no slats in the walls where a tiny hoof could get stuck and no hooks to scratch or damage the unwary baby. Judy had showed Carole how even the slightest mistake could hurt a newborn.

Although she was a doctor, Judy's uniform consisted of soft blue jeans, a cool cotton blouse, and leather boots. She was a familiar sight throughout the county, driving along the country roads—sometimes at breakneck speed—in her light blue pickup truck, with a camper on the back to hold the oversize medical equipment she needed for her oversize patients.

Sometimes, Carole could picture herself in such a rig, taking emergency calls on the cellular phone in the truck's cab. She'd rush to the side of a colicky mare, or clear up a skin infection on a jumper, or calm a nervous mother-to-be, as Judy was doing now.

And sometimes Carole saw herself only as the owner of the mare, or the jumper, or the mother-to-be. Carole didn't know exactly how she was going to work with horses when she grew up—whether as an owner, trainer, breeder, or vet—but whatever she did, she knew it would always involve horses. Until she made up her mind, she wanted to learn everything she possibly could.

Delilah's foal was the most exciting thing that had ever happened to her as a rider. Not only had Cobalt been the horse of her dreams, until his tragic death, but Delilah was the stable horse she had always ridden. She knew Delilah better than she knew any other horse. Delilah trusted her. And Max had already asked her if she would help raise and train the foal. She hadn't had to think twice to answer that question.

"There are signs that she's about to deliver her foal," Judy explained.

"Is it that soon?"

"Well, maybe," Judy told her. "Mares—particularly ones foaling for the first time—can be pretty unpredictable. We have to watch them very closely. From the look of this one now, I'd say she'll deliver sometime in the next three weeks."

"How do you know?" Carole asked, fascinated.

Judy showed her where the foal lay in the mare's huge belly. Then she showed her the mare's enlarged udder, already filling with milk to be ready when her newborn was hungry for the first time. "See, these are signs that we're not far off. But she's not ready yet. I really don't expect the foal for at least two weeks, and it could be four or five."

"Should somebody be staying with her now? I mean, I could bring in my sleeping bag and stay with her, like, just in case—"

"No, not yet," Judy said, smiling at Carole. "The time will come, but it's not yet. I'll let you know—when Delilah tells me." Just then, the phone in Judy's truck rang. While Judy answered the call, Carole stood at the door to Delilah's stall, patting the horse's nose and whispering reassuring words in her big, soft ears. Delilah eyed Carole calmly. Then, because the foal inside her was growing at a tremendous rate, Delilah turned to the thing that interested her most these days—fresh hay—and began eating. Carole wandered outside and found Judy cramming the last of her equipment back in her truck.

"Emergency?" Carole asked with concern.

"The big bay mare at Cloverleaf is about to foal. She had us all in a tither with her last foal, so I want to be cautious this time. Say, you want to come along? You might even be some help. I'll drive you home afterward. You can call your dad on my phone here. . . ."

Without a second's thought, Carole yanked open the door on the passenger side of the blue pickup and jumped in.

"You *bet!*" she said. As soon as the door slammed, Judy turned on the engine and pulled out of the drive at Pine Hollow. When they roared past one of the town's police cars a few minutes later, they were going fifty in a thirty-five-mile-per-hour speed zone. Judy waved at the officer in the car.

"Isn't he going to give you a ticket?" Carole asked.

"That's Jack Miller," Judy said, as if it were an explanation. "He's got a pony for his kids. Jingles nearly died last year with a deep cut he got from a barbed-wire fence. Jack knows why I drive fast."

Carole gripped the armrest and watched the countryside fly by. She was too excited to be nervous anyway.

AT HOME IN her own room, Lisa got ready for her surprise for The Saddle Club. She expected to spend most of the weekend working on it. Her desk, almost unused since school had closed for the summer, was clear and waiting. She took out a notebook she'd bought to write the constitution in. The clean white pages and neat blue lines, edged on the left with a red vertical border, were inviting. She selected a sharp-pointed pen from the mug on her desk. She adjusted her chair. She turned on the three-way lamp.

THE SADDLE CLUB

she wrote.

But how was it to begin?

There was a familiar scratching at her door. Her dog, a golden Lhasa apso named Dolly, wanted to come in. Lisa opened the door and patted Dolly, scratching her neck just where she liked it the most. The fluffy dog scampered up onto the upholstered chair next to the window. Lisa watched while Dolly circled exactly three times and then settled down for a nap. She always circled three times and it always fascinated Lisa. Dolly was such a creature of habit. But then, so was Lisa. They were a good pair.

Lisa sat down in her chair again, adjusting the light.

Rules

she wrote.

We, the members of The Saddle Club, in order to form a more perfect union . . .

Lisa groaned at the familiarity of those words. Plagiarism was no way to start a good club! She really needed to organize her thoughts before she began making up the rules. So, she jotted down a list of subjects for the rules.

> meetings
> dues
> officers
> projects
> requirements for membership
> new members
> purpose

That was the start she needed. Lisa began outlining the regulations under each of the categories she'd created and soon her pen was moving quickly across the page.

When Dolly scratched at the inside of the door to signal that it was time to go outside for a walk, Lisa was surprised to see that an hour had passed. She glanced at her notebook. She'd filled eight pages with outlines and rules.

Now, that was progress!

STEVIE DASHED UP the stairs to her room. She dumped her boots and her riding hat in the general vicinity of a chair and yanked her closet door open.

"I'm sure it's still here," she mumbled as she burrowed into the back of her less-than-perfectly-organized closet. "I *couldn't* have thrown it away." She grabbed the handle of an umbrella with four broken ribs. That wasn't what she wanted. She shoved it back into a corner. "*Could* Mom have . . . ?" Then she extracted what turned out to be a drum majorette's baton. That wasn't what she wanted at all. She tossed that next to the umbrella. But maybe it had possibilities for the games. She decided to consider it later.

Then, at last, her hand closed on the rounded object she sought. She tugged at it gently, trying not to topple the rest of the stuff in the closet. Finally, Stevie emerged triumphantly from her closet clutching a Hula-Hoop.

"Perfect!" she said proudly. Her father had bought it for her at a garage sale a year ago. He'd thought it was terribly funny to find one of those big plastic hoops that had been all the rage when her parents were kids. Stevie had thought this toy was fairly dumb until now. Now all she had to do was to figure out how to use a Hula-Hoop while riding a horse. She put it over her head and tried to get it to circle her waist. The thing quickly clattered to the floor. That didn't matter, though, because it would be impossible to hula on horseback. But could she swing it around on, say, her forearm without spooking the horse?

She got the hoop to circle her forearm. She tried to imagine being a horse, watching the spinning hoop, and decided she wasn't upset by it—even when it upset a lampshade. Then she decided that wasn't really an objective test.

"What are you doing?" asked her twin brother, Alex, opening the door. "I mean, are you into busting up furniture now?"

"No, I'm just—hey, you can help me. Come on in here." She grabbed his arm and pulled him into her room. "I really need help, see. It's for the gymkhana," she began, but he interrupted her.

"Gym-what?" he asked.

"The gymkhana. It's for Pine Hollow—a tournament of fun, silly games you play on horseback."

"Not me, Sis," Alex said. "I don't know anything about horses, you know that. And, anyway, I'm on my way over to Ron Ziegler's house. His little brothers got a Laser Tag for their birthday, but they've gone to a friend's house this afternoon, so Ron and I—"

"Laser Tag! That's perfect!" Stevie shouted. She'd never actually played it, but she knew it was an electronic game of tag with guns that shot light beams at a vest, which lit up when the beam hit its target. It seemed like a perfect gymkhana game. "I've *got* to borrow it."

"What do you mean you've got to borrow it? It belongs to Ron's little brothers, and you know what monsters they are. If you want to borrow something from them, in the first place, you're crazy, but in the second place, *you* ask them."

"Oh, come on, Alex," Stevie said in her sweetest, most appealing twin-sister voice, ignoring the phone as it began to ring. "You've just got to get them to let me use it—"

"Stevie, phone call!" her brother Chad yelled up the stairs.

She walked to the door and opened it. Looking down toward Chad at the foot of the stairs, she asked, "Who is it?"

"I dunno," he informed her.

"I'll be right there," she told Chad. "But first . . ." She turned to talk to Alex again, but he'd escaped through the other door to her room while she was talking with Chad. She stepped to her window, and saw him jogging across their lawn. She raised the sash. "Come on, Alex, you've only got to *ask* them for me!" she called after him. He continued on his way, pretending not to hear her.

Stevie sighed and picked up the phone on her bedside table—a major, long-hoped-for twelfth birthday present (though at that moment, she wished she'd gotten Laser Tag).

"Hullo?"

"Where were you? What took you so long to answer?" Carole asked her over the phone.

"Oh, it's my dumb brother," Stevie explained. "I've just got to borrow a Laser Tag set, and he won't ask his best friend—well, actually it's his little brothers—to lend it to me. I mean, it'll be fantastic. Don't you think so?"

"Well, I guess it's a pretty good game," Carole said, "but I never much wanted to play it myself."

"It's for the gymkhana!" Stevie said. "Oh, but I didn't get a chance to tell you about it, did I?"

"Nope," Carole said just a little sarcastically, but Stevie didn't notice.

"Well, that's what Max wanted to see me about. We're going to have a gymkhana and he wants me to come up with all kinds of neat games for it. Mrs. Reg just suggested an egg-in-a-spoon race and a rope race, but I want something more exciting than that stuff.

Can you think of anything better than Laser Tag on horseback?"

"I guess that would be fun," Carole told her.

"You guess? Is that all you can say? It would be the best thing in the world!"

"No, *I* just saw the best thing in the world," Carole said. "I just saw a newborn foal."

Suddenly, gymkhanas didn't seem so all-important to Stevie. "Delilah had the foal already?"

"Not yet. This was a mare at Cloverleaf. I went over there with Judy because the trainer called while Judy was visiting Delilah. By the time we got to Cloverleaf, the foal was born, but we got to watch her nursing for the first time. You can't imagine how cute she was! She's a little bay filly—you know, brown with a black mane and tail—but she's got these gigantic ears and long spindly legs with big knobby knees."

Stevie could picture the newborn foal. She knew it was a female because Carole had called it a filly. Males were called colts. Stevie had seen pictures of foals less than an hour old struggling to their feet for their first meals, short tails swishing tentatively. "Oh, she must be so cute!" Stevie said. "Hey, can we visit her tomorrow?"

"Well, I don't know about that," Carole told her. "Newborn foals are very delicate. Judy said the trainer is going to have to keep almost constant watch for the next couple of days. You can't believe the number of diseases foals can get right after they're born—"

"Well, I'm not going to give her any germs, if that's what you're scared of," Stevie said. She was hurt that Carole would think she was any less able to be careful around a newborn than Carole herself would be.

"Well, it's not just that," Carole protested. "I mean, it was sort of a special thing that I got to be there and I wouldn't want Judy to think that just anybody could crowd into the stable, you know what I mean?" Carole asked.

There was a part of Stevie that did know what Carole meant—or at least understood why she wanted to be special. But most of her was just hurt by the implication that she would upset the foal while Carole wouldn't. That was like Carole—trying to share, but winding up bragging instead. "How come you're less of a 'just anybody' than I am?" Stevie asked suspiciously.

"Oh, I didn't mean it that way, Stevie," Carole said quickly. "It's just that, well, I don't know, I sort of felt, like I was the luckiest person in the world to be there. The whole time, I was thinking how great it would be if you and Lisa could be there, too. But this wasn't our horse or our stable. I was just kind of an uninvited guest. So, I was afraid if I asked to invite somebody else, they'd tell me to go away. Does that make sense?"

"Just a little," Stevie conceded. She was sure, though, that if she had been there, she would have telephoned her best friends and told them to come right away. Carole could be a little timid. Nobody ever accused Stevie of that. "You'll be sure to let us know if Delilah gets ready to deliver, won't you?" Stevie asked.

"I mean, Lisa and I won't be uninvited guests *then*, will we?"

"Of course I'll call you. And you can bet I'll be there," Carole told her. "As soon as Judy says Delilah's getting ready to deliver, I'm moving into the stable. Dad already got me a cot from the base, and a sleeping bag and a bunch of camping stuff so I won't have to leave Delilah's side. I wouldn't miss this for the world! And since I'll be there, you'll be there. Lisa, too. It's a promise."

Stevie knew she meant that. When it came to horses, Carole could be just as stubborn and determined as Stevie was—maybe even more so.

"Okay, then in the meantime, I'm going to be very busy with this gymkhana. I've never been in one. Have you?" Stevie asked.

"Oh, sure. We had one at the last base Dad was stationed at. It was fun. We had a rope race where you had to hold a rope with your partner and go around the poles. Then in another race, you had to hold an egg on a spoon."

"Oh, those are the ordinary kinds of races Mrs. Reg told me about," Stevie said. "I'm trying to do something a little different—I want this to be the *best*! That's why I want to borrow the Laser Tag. And, you know what I found that I think will be perfect, but I'm just not exactly sure how? A Hula-Hoop! Say, your dad has all kinds of fifties stuff. Do you think he has a Hula-Hoop somewhere?"

"I'll ask him," Carole said without enthusiasm. "But I don't remember seeing anything like that. Oh, he's at the door now. Gotta go. I want to tell him about the foal."

"Don't forget to ask about the Hula-Hoop, huh?" Stevie reminded her.

"Uh, sure," Carole said, but she didn't sound sure, and that irritated Stevie. "Bye."

Stevie stared at her phone for a while after she'd hung up. It had been a peculiarly unsatisfying phone call from her best friend. Well, one of her best friends. She picked up the phone to call Lisa.

A FEW BLOCKS away, Lisa was grinning with pride. She leaned back, lifting the front legs of her chair off the floor. She held a sheaf of papers filled with her tidy handwriting in front of her. The job was almost complete now. She only had to type the rules on her mother's computer and she'd be able to make as many copies as she needed.

She had decided to make five rules for each section of the rule book. The rule book itself began with the statement of purpose. That had taken her the most time. It read: "The purpose of The Saddle Club is to increase the knowledge and enjoyment of horseback riding for its members." For a while, she'd thought of just putting, "The purpose of The Saddle Club is threefold: horses, horses, and horses," but that seemed silly. Anyway, once she knew what her purpose was, the rules were easy.

Regular meetings would be held once a week, on Thursdays from three to five o'clock. Members had to come to meetings, but if they couldn't, they could miss up to one a month. If they missed any more, they'd have to pay fines of one dollar per missed meeting. If they missed three in a row, they could be voted out by other members. If they were late to meetings, they'd be fined twenty-five cents for each quarter hour they were late. Meetings would follow the standard *Rules of Order.*

Officers would be elected by the members. There would be a president, vice president, and secretary-treasurer.

Lisa figured Carole would be the president because she was the best rider. Stevie would be the vice president because she was the next-best rider and she was too disorganized to be the secretary-treasurer. Lisa herself would be the secretary-treasurer.

There were eight more pages of rules, including sections on projects, new members, and dues, all neatly detailing every aspect of The Saddle Club. Lisa had spent a lot of time on the section on projects, since one of the things members had to do was to help others in the Club. After all, the Club had been formed when she and Carole had pitched in to help Stevie with her math project for school.

She was very proud of what she'd done. She was sure Carole and Stevie would be, too. In fact, she was about to call one of them when the phone rang. It was Stevie calling her.

"Oh, I was just going to call you," Lisa said.

"I wanted to tell you what Max said to me," Stevie explained. "He wants *me* to plan a gymkhana for every afternoon of the three-day event next month. Can you believe it?"

"What's a gymkhana?" Lisa asked. Stevie explained about the games and races she was working on.

"Oh, like relay races, huh? I know a neat race you can do carrying an egg in a spoon. I bet that would be fun on a horse."

"That's the oldest race in the book," Stevie said. "I want to come up with some new things. This time it's going to be more fun than ever. That's why Max asked *me* to do it. See, he knows he can count on me to be outrageous."

"I guess that's true," Lisa agreed, but she really didn't see anything wrong with carrying an egg in a spoon. It certainly wouldn't be easy on a horse. "Well, I've been busy, too," Lisa said, trying to change the subject to one more to her liking. "I've been working on a Saddle Club project."

"Is there one?" Stevie asked.

"Well, there's our new set of rules and regulations," Lisa said proudly. She waited for Stevie to be impressed, but she was soon disappointed.

"You mean like rules for the games I'm making up?" Stevie asked.

"No, rules for the Club," Lisa went on. "You know how frustrated we always are when we have a meeting and then it's over and we haven't really accomplished anything? Now we can accomplish things. Wait'll you see—"

"Rules aren't my strong point," Stevie told Lisa.

"Well, you just don't like the dumb rules they have at school and the strict ones Max makes up. These are *good* rules. They're just absolutely going to *make* The Saddle Club. Now, finally, we're going to be a *real* club."

"We weren't already a *real* club?" Stevie wondered.

"Not really. At least, not until now. Wait till you see," Lisa said again.

"And wait'll you see what wonderful and outrageous games I come up with!"

"See you Monday," Lisa told her.

"Right," Stevie said.

Lisa wasn't awfully surprised that Stevie was lukewarm about her project. She'd see, though, Lisa was sure, how much better and more fun it would be to have a club that really was a club. It just wasn't the sort of thing Stevie would be excited about right away. She didn't think much of rules. But Carole, on the other hand, would be excited about it all.

"OH, DAD, YOU can't imagine how wonderful it was!" Carole cooed from the couch in the living room.

"I think I can, honey," Colonel Hanson told his daughter. He peered around the corner at her from the kitchen. "Birth is probably the most exciting thing in the world."

31

"I was right next to Judy the whole time, too," Carole continued. "I watched her examine the mare and the filly. The little baby kept trying to nip at her hands. I think she was looking for more milk!"

Carole was practically exploding with excitment and wanted to share every detail with her father. Stevie certainly hadn't been a satisfactory audience—too involved with her games. A gymkhana would be fun, to be sure, but it wasn't in the same league as a newborn foal.

The phone rang. Carole dashed into the kitchen. Maybe it was about Delilah, she thought. She picked up the receiver from just beneath her father's hand. He stepped back, amused.

"Oh, it's you, Lisa," Carole said, disappointment in her voice.

Of course Carole had been about to call Lisa and tell her about the foal, but before she could even get into it, Lisa began telling her about rules and The Saddle Club. Carole's mind was so focused on the newborn foal that she really couldn't make much sense of Lisa's excitement. It seemed an awful lot like Stevie and the gymkhana. It was clear to Carole that this was no time to try to talk to Lisa about the foal. It would be better to tell her father the rest of the story.

"Gee, Lisa, that sounds great," Carole said, mustering all the sincerity she could find for whatever Lisa was talking about. "But I'm kind of busy with my dad now. Mind if we talk about this on Monday?"

Quickly, the phone conversation ended. For a moment Carole paused to wonder what Lisa had been talking about. Rules? The Club didn't have any rules. Right then, it didn't really matter to Carole anyway. All she could think about was the foal.

THE THING ABOUT being mad at Stevie and Carole was that Lisa couldn't be mad at them while they were at class. They all had too much fun together when they were riding.

As soon as the three of them were on their horses on Monday morning, all the irritations from Friday were gone. It was a new week, a fresh start.

All twelve of the stable's summer-camp students were in the class, which took place in the outdoor ring. The ring, at the back of the stable, was really a large rectangle, sixty by eighty meters. Max stood in the center and barked orders at his eager students.

"Today, we're going to try something a little different," Max began. "I'm thinking of starting a drill team. This isn't exactly a tryout, but I want to see how well each of you can follow the orders and control your horse. Both of those are extremely important for drill work."

Lisa's heart sank. She was sure she didn't have the knowledge or experience to be able to do this at all. She'd seen drill teams doing their exercises. In fact, she'd seen an exhibition of it on cable television not long ago. It had looked just about impossible, considering the skill needed for such precision, but it also had looked wonderful. Lisa's fear was so mixed up with her excitement that she wasn't sure which she should be feeling. She looked over at Stevie and Carole, paired together on the other side of the ring. The looks on their faces answered the question for her: She should be excited.

"Listen up!" Max called. "I want a single line, evenly spaced. Get your horses trotting and maintain a trot throughout this exercise."

Usually Max didn't use a riding crop when he was teaching, but today he was strutting around, slapping the riding crop against his leg and the palm of his hand. He looked very stern. It made Lisa more nervous than usual.

"Up! Down! Up! Down! Pay attention, now, Lisa. You know how to post better than that!" Max yelled as they all started trotting.

So even when Max was looking like a movie director, he was still paying attention to every single mistake Lisa could make. Her heart sank. If she couldn't keep up with his instructions, she'd never make the drill team!

"Heels down!" Lisa pushed down on her heels as hard as possible. "Much better now, Betsy," Max continued. "But you must *remember* to keep your heels down." Lisa realized that she was getting so paranoid that she assumed Max was *always* criticizing her. "Look at Lisa, Betsy," he said. "She's got her heels way down. You want yours like that, too." Lisa smiled to herself.

Quickly, however, she found that sitting properly on her horse, with her heels down, wasn't going to be her only problem. The real trick of this exercise was to keep her horse at a dead-even pace—and aligned with all the other horses. If one horse speeded up, its rider had to slow it down, or everyone *else* had to speed up. The most important thing was unison.

"Now, down to a walk," Max said. Lisa reined in on Pepper. He seemed only too happy to walk. She patted his neck, rewarding him for keeping up his trot so nicely. "We'll try this once at a walk, and then we'll be back trotting," Max said. Then he described how they were to walk their horses in a figure eight across the center of the ring, alternating sides at the crossing point in the middle of the eight. If they messed up and let more than one horse pass at a time, the figure would be uneven.

Lisa was sure she'd be the one to mess it up. That made her all the more determined to do it right.

She was following Betsy Cavanaugh, who still wasn't sitting properly on her horse, Barq. He could tell it, too, and was giving her trouble, breaking gait and sort of sidling off course.

"Look straight ahead, Betsy," Max said. Betsy turned her head and focused on her lane with determination. In response, her horse got back where she wanted him. But Lisa was still worried; if Betsy lost her concentration, it could make Lisa mess up as well.

And, of course, it happened. When Betsy got to the cross in the eight, she was so busy looking to her right to see if the other horse was coming that Barq, confused by her different signals, came to a sudden halt. Two horses went past him before she could get him back into gear and across the middle of the eight.

Lisa wasted no time in making up her mind. She urged Pepper in front of the next horse—Comanche, with Stevie on board—and hurried across after Betsy. Lisa's maneuver left Stevie groaning at her, since she was all ready to go across the path, but it kept the figure eight in balance, with six horses on each half.

"Nice work, Lisa," Max said. "When one person makes a mistake, everybody *else* has to correct it."

Did she hear it right? Max was actually praising her!

"Sorry, Lisa," Betsy called over her shoulder. "I'm just having a terrible time with Barq today—or else it's me. I don't know."

Lisa knew. It had clearly been Betsy's fault, but since Max had lavished her with praise, she didn't want to be mean to Betsy. "No problem, Betsy," Lisa said magnanimously. "Horses have bad days, too, just like people."

"Nice work," Max said to the entire class at the end of the lesson. "If you all enjoyed that, we can do more of it. Who thought it was fun?"

Lisa glanced around at her classmates. Most of them looked sort of frustrated and tired. It was true that it had been a tough lesson. Max had shouted a lot—and not just at Betsy. Still, it had been fun for Lisa, and *very* satisfying when she'd succeeded. Lisa put her hand up.

To her surprise, only two other hands went up— Stevie's and Carole's. For a second, Lisa thought Max was trying to hide a smile. Then he spoke. "Okay, if you three enjoyed it, then I think it would be a good idea for you to work on drills. We'll have additional classes Monday, Wednesday, and Friday at three. Now, pair up, walk your horses around the circle until they've cooled down, then break for lunch. At two o'clock this afternoon, we're going to work on grooming, so put your horses in their stalls for now, untack them, and give them fresh water and hay. *Dis-missed!!*"

"Wasn't that just great?" Stevie asked Carole as the two of them led their horses to their stalls. "I mean, it's like almost a perfect combination of the things I enjoy about riding—equitation and dressage. The only thing missing is jumping and, I guess, cross-country, and racing, and uh, well, check that. What I enjoy about riding is *everything*! Drill work included."

"It's neat," Carole agreed. "Since I lived on Marine Corps bases for ten years, I've seen an awful lot of drill work—mostly on foot, you know, like parades. This is really the first time I've gotten to do it, unless you count the time my Girl Scout troop marched in the Marine Corps Birthday Parade a couple of years ago."

"I don't think that's exactly the same thing," Stevie said, laughing.

"Me neither." Carole grinned. "It's much more fun on horseback. And I just knew when Max asked who had liked it that it would be the three of us."

"Yeah, I'm glad about that," Stevie agreed. "After all, we are The Saddle Club."

"You going to have lunch now?" Carole asked.

"No, I forgot my sandwich. It doesn't matter, though. I've got something I have to work on as soon as I untack Comanche."

"If you're in such a rush, I'll untack him for you," Carole offered.

"Would you?"

"Sure I would," Carole told her, reaching for the reins. Gladly, Stevie relinquished them.

"See you later," she said, dashing off to the tack room.

Carole really didn't mind at all. She'd rather spend time with horses than doing almost anything. Besides, it would make the time pass faster until Judy came to check Delilah for the day.

LATER, LISA FOUND Carole sitting on a knoll by the paddock where Delilah was being kept until she foaled. It was next to her foaling stall, in sight of the office so she could be watched all the time. Carole was eating her sandwich and drinking her soda, but one hundred percent of her attention was on Delilah.

"How's she doing?" Lisa asked as she sat down beside her friend.

"Judy says she's doing just fine. You always have to be concerned about a mare with her first foal, but Judy says Delilah seems to be a good mother. She eats her special mash and she's resting a lot. Judy says it should be just fine."

"She seems to be kind of listless," Lisa said, observing how slowly Delilah walked.

"That's just because she's gotten so big now that it's almost hard for her to walk. But Judy says she'll be back in good shape within a few weeks after the birth. She'll be running in the paddock with her foal and that'll slim her right down again. She'll be her old self in no time. Isn't that amazing?"

For a second, Lisa wondered if she was really talking to Carole—or to Judy. Then she remembered why she particularly wanted to see Carole.

"I have your set of rules," Lisa told her. She had spent hours over the weekend working on her mother's computer, inputting everything on the word processor. Her mother had helped her, and when they'd finally printed it all out, it was beautiful—as pretty as a term paper, Lisa thought.

"What rules?" Carole asked.

"The Saddle Club rules," Lisa said, containing her impatience. "Remember, I told you about them Friday when I called? I know you were busy, but I'm sure I told you about all this work I'd done so we could have a *real* club. Remember?"

"Oh, yeah," Carole said vaguely, taking the papers from Lisa's hand. "I'll read them later, okay?"

"Okay," Lisa agreed. "And we'll have a meeting on Thursday afternoon after class, at TD's, to make any changes you guys want. Then we can ratify them. That means make them official."

"Thursday," Carole echoed. "Okay. Look at the way she's eating now." Lisa realized Carole was talking about Delilah again. "It's like she's hungry all the time. And Judy says that's good. She needs fresh hay and fresh water constantly. I'm going to muck out her stall before Judy gets here. Oh, how I love doing things for that horse!"

Lisa liked to do things for horses too, but mucking out stalls wasn't high on her list. "I've got to find Stevie. Know where she is?"

"She was in an awful hurry right after class, but I don't know where she went. Try the indoor ring. She was headed in that direction."

"See you," Lisa said, but she really didn't think her friend heard her at all. Carole was already headed for Delilah's stall. Lisa made her way down the knoll and into the stable. It seemed terribly dark inside, in comparison to the bright summer sunshine. They were spending almost all of their riding time outdoors, mostly in the ring, and sometimes on the trails. It was nice to be out in the fresh air. The class only used the cramped indoor ring on rainy days. It seemed a long time since Lisa had taken her first lesson in that ring.

Lisa passed the tack room and peered into the indoor ring. There was Stevie. She'd borrowed a pony. Lisa knew that any horse less than four feet ten inches tall at the withers was called a pony. A lot of mounted games took place on ponies because the ponies were what the little kids could ride. Stevie, it seemed, was trying to determine whether a pony could do one of the games she was planning.

While Lisa watched, Stevie climbed onto Nickel, a pretty silver-colored pony. She held a Hula-Hoop in her right hand. She put the hoop around her right arm and began trying to get it to swing around her arm. It did just fine when it was *up,* but as soon as it came *down,* it smacked into the soft dirt and bounced off her arm. It wasn't working at all. The pony was just too short. She tried swinging it over her head, but right away, it got tangled in her hard hat. Angrily, Stevie threw the thing across the ring.

Next, Lisa watched her take a spoon with a marshmallow on it, climb on Nickel, and begin galloping across the ring. The marshmallow fell off right away. Stevie dismounted, picked it up, and climbed up again. This time the marshmallow fell off before she even got back in the saddle. She picked it up a third time, mashed it into the spoon so it was more of a glob than a marshmallow, climbed into the saddle, and was off. The only problem was that when she got to the end of the ring, where there was a bucket, she couldn't get the gooey marshmallow out of the spoon and into the bucket. After the third try at shaking it loose, she threw *that* across the ring as well, so it landed near the abandoned Hula-Hoop.

Something told Lisa this was no time to try to talk to Stevie. As quietly as she had come, she left, going into the tack room. There, she quickly spotted Stevie's shoes. She rolled up a copy of the rules and stuck it into one of Stevie's shoes, leaving a note about the Thursday meeting at TD's.

Stevie would find the note there and they could talk about the new rules on Thursday at TD's. She was sure Stevie would be in a better mood by then. Well, pretty sure.

Lisa fetched her own sandwich and soda from the refrigerator and looked for a place to eat. Just as she stepped into the stall area, she saw Estelle Duval, the new French girl, eating alone.

"Can I sit down?" Lisa asked.

"*Mais, oui,*" Estelle said. "Of course."

Lisa just loved the sound of her accent.

5

ON THURSDAY AFTERNOON, Lisa couldn't find Stevie and Carole after camp was over. It was time for The Saddle Club meeting at TD's—their favorite ice cream store, in the nearby shopping center—and it was an important meeting, too. It was the meeting Lisa had called so they could discuss and approve all the rules she'd written.

When she couldn't find her friends, Lisa decided they must have left for TD's, thinking *she'd* already gone. She changed into her jeans and street shoes and set out for the shopping center, a little annoyed to have been left behind.

As soon as she crossed the roadway, Lisa spotted Estelle walking in the same direction she was headed. She and Estelle had eaten lunch together two days in a row and Lisa was really getting to like her. She was so chic, so sophisticated, so nice!

It surprised Lisa that Estelle seemed to want to be her friend. After all, Estelle had told her she had been riding since she was a toddler, and most of the friends she talked about were really fancy people, like princes and counts and children of diplomats. She'd been to school in several different countries and spoke four languages. Lisa only spoke English, a few words of French, and pig latin!

"Hey, Estelle! Wait up!" Lisa called, and jogged up to the French girl. "Which way are you going?" she asked.

"I'm going to the little shopping center," Estelle told her. "I wanted to see if there is a jewelry store there. I have a necklace that needs to have a new gold chain."

"Well, I'm going that way, too, though I don't have to buy any jewelry today," Lisa joked. Then she explained she was meeting friends at TD's. "You were having some trouble today on Nero, weren't you?" she asked after a moment as they continued on their way.

"Oh?" Estelle said. She seemed to be surprised that Lisa had noticed, but the fact was that everybody had noticed. Nero had ended up doing almost exactly what he'd wanted to do all through the class. That was really bad. Lisa had been taught from her very first lesson that a rider had to be the one in control, and the horse needed to know it.

"Nero was in such a bad mood!" Estelle explained. "You see, I am much more used to my own horse,

Napoleon. He would never behave that way."

"Your own horse!" Lisa exclaimed. "And you had to leave him in France, I guess. You must miss him a lot."

"I certainly do. He's a white horse, a beautiful stallion. He was a gift to me from a friend of my father's— the ambassador," she explained. "But I have had him since my seventh birthday. I rode him for hours that day, and every day since, when I am at home. He never acted so naughty like Nero was today."

"I thought you lived in the city of Paris. Do you keep him in the city?" Lisa asked, recalling her earlier conversations with Estelle.

"Oh—uh, no, but he is kept at our country home in Normandy, northwest of Paris. We go there on weekends and for vacations. That's when I ride him. At other times, the stable manager exercises him for me, you see?"

Lisa *did* see. Her mind's eye built a spacious country estate with a large barn and rolling hills where horses frolicked gracefully through the spring flowers in the pastures. Liveried staff tended to the home while the Duvals were in Paris, and catered to their every whim when they returned to the country. It seemed so incredibly elegant that Lisa could hardly believe it was true.

"You know, Estelle, I haven't been riding very long," Lisa explained. "I just started a few months ago. I really love it, though, and every time I hear about somebody like you, who has been riding since she was really little, well, it makes me wish I'd started it a long time ago, too. I hate to think of all the wonderful rides I missed!"

"But Lisa, all the rides are *not* wonderful," Estelle corrected her.

"You mean like all the trouble you had with Nero today?"

"Well, that too, but let me tell you about the pony I had *before* Napoleon. That one was a mare. Her name was Étoile—French for 'star' because of the perfect five-pointed star on her forehead. But it was the only perfect thing about her. One day I was riding her. I was just a little girl then, of course. By mistake, I happened to tug at her mane when I was standing up in the saddle, trying to get my balance. It must have hurt her terribly, for right away, she began trying to kick at me with her hind foot. I pulled the reins to make her stop. Then I climbed down from her saddle right there in the middle of the field, and I told Maman I was never going to ride the beast again!"

Estelle laughed so hard at the story that Lisa began laughing, too. She could just see the stubborn child informing her mother she was through. But she couldn't see herself trying the same thing with Max! Max certainly wouldn't force people to ride if they didn't enjoy it. But there was no way he would let somebody quit just because one bad thing happened— even a nasty fall. Lisa decided it was a good thing for Estelle that Max wasn't her mother.

The two girls strolled across the parking lot of the little shopping center. It wasn't really a mall. It only boasted a supermarket, a few shoe stores, a drugstore, a record store, a jewelry store, and the ice cream parlor, TD's. If what you wanted after riding class was an ice-cream sundae, there was no place better than TD's. Lisa paused at TD's, but there was no sign of Stevie or Carole. Realizing they must have been delayed, she continued to walk with Estelle.

Together, the girls went into the jewelry store. Estelle spoke with the salesman for a long time, though Lisa couldn't hear what she was saying. Lisa loved jewelry and always had fun looking at it. She could imagine a day when she might have long conversations with jewelers the way Estelle was, but for now, she satisfied herself with glancing at the costume jewelry section. She looked at the pins under the glass counter. There, in the center, was a pin with the silhouette of a horse head superimposed on a horseshoe. The horse's ears were perked alertly, his mane brushed slightly by the wind. The whole effect was so pretty that it nearly took Lisa's breath away. Somehow, that pin seemed to represent everything Lisa loved about horses. If only . . .

"Oh, this man can't help me at all," Estelle whined, interrupting Lisa's thoughts. "I have wasted my time!"

"Not exactly," Lisa consoled her, turning from the showcase with the horse-head pin. "We got to walk together and have a nice talk."

"Let's get out of here," Estelle said, leading Lisa back onto the shopping center sidewalk. "You have to meet your friends now, no?"

"Oh, yes," Lisa said, heading for TD's. But even before she entered the ice cream shop, she could see through the window that neither Stevie nor Carole was there yet. She wondered what had happened. How could she have missed them at Pine Hollow? She was just about certain they'd gone by the time she left.

"What's the matter, Lisa?" Estelle asked.

"I'm looking for Stevie and Carole," she explained. "We were supposed to meet here. I'm sure they'd left Pine Hollow by the time I did, so where are they?"

"Carole Hanson and Stevie Lake?" Estelle asked. Lisa nodded. "But I saw them go," Estelle said. "Carole, she went off in the truck with that woman doctor, Judy is her name? And, then, Stevie, she saddled up the pony, Nickel, and was taking him out into the field. She had the most tremendous bag full of things, but I don't know what was in it."

Lisa got a deep sinking feeling. It was clear that both Carole and Stevie had completely forgotten The Club meeting they were supposed to have. Each was so wrapped up in her own special project that she didn't even remember *Lisa's* special project! Lisa was just about to explode with anger and hurt. How could her best friends let her down?

"So look at us now," Estelle said brightly. "You came here to meet your friends, but they're not coming. I came here to go to the jewelry store, but they did not have what I wanted! We are in the same pair of shoes!"

Lisa laughed at Estelle's joke and she was glad for it. She swallowed hard and scrunched her eyes to hide any possible tears. "Well, since neither of our plans worked out, how about some ice cream?"

"That's a great idea," Estelle agreed, and together they headed for TD's.

Within a few minutes, they'd found a table and ordered their sundaes. Lisa was surprised to learn that Estelle wasn't familiar with all the possibilities at an ice cream parlor.

"Don't you have ice cream in France?" she asked.

"Of course we do, but we don't have it so fancy as you do here—and I don't know what these things are." She lifted the menu and pointed. "Like what's this 'marshmallow fluff'?"

The way she said *fluff* made it sound more like *floof*. Lisa laughed.

Estelle seemed a little hurt. "I'm sorry," Lisa said quickly. "It's just that you make it sound so much better than it is! But it's pronounced *fluff*," she said, emphasizing the short *u*. Estelle tried it again and got it right. Lisa told her what it was.

"But it must be marvelous—sort of like meringue, eh?"

"Want to try it? They can add it on top of your hot fudge."

Estelle's eyes sparkled at the idea. Lisa stepped over to the counter and asked the waitress to add marshmallow fluff to one of the sundaes. Then she returned and the two girls talked.

Lisa found that talking to Estelle was fun. She had done so many exciting things in her life, and lived in so many interesting places, that Lisa was almost jeal-ous.

"Did I tell you about the princess who used to be in my class at boarding school?"

"Princess? A *real* princess?" Estelle nodded. "What country?" Lisa asked breathlessly.

"Oh, goodness, I'm not sure I remember. One of those small ones, you know?" Estelle told her.

Lisa didn't know, but she told Estelle she did. It was one thing if a person needed to know what marsh-mallow fluff was. Anybody could need to know about that. But it was another thing altogether to need to be told about entire countries, even small ones. Lisa de-cided to cling to her ignorance rather than exhibit it.

Estelle went on to tell a story about how this girl had invited everybody in the class to her parents' castle for the weekend, but it turned out that it was such a small estate that there wasn't room in the castle for all the girls to have their own rooms. As the tale unfolded, Lisa was simply swept away. To her, it was like a movie come alive, a dream come true. She just loved listen-ing to Estelle's stories. What a life she'd lived—and how lucky Lisa was even to know her.

Before she knew it, she had an empty sundae dish in front of her, and the clock on the wall told her it was time to get home.

"I've got to go," she said. "My mom will be expect-ing me."

"Me too," Estelle told her. "My chauffeur is picking

me up here in a little while. Would you like a ride home?"

Lisa was tempted. Really tempted. But her house was only a short walk and she really couldn't wait any longer. "Another time," she said.

They paid their check and left TD's. Lisa set off for home at a quick pace. She'd had such a nice time with Estelle that, for an hour, she'd completely forgotten about Carole and Stevie and how much they had hurt her. She'd forgotten about how much she'd been looking forward to discussing her rules with them. Talking to Estelle was like being swept away in the fantasy land of a wonderful book. Everything about her was so different, and so exciting!

Lisa's copy of the Club's rules was in her tote bag. She hadn't even taken it out at TD's because there hadn't been a meeting.

But there *had* been, she told herself. She'd called a meeting at TD's and just because two people hadn't showed up it didn't mean there hadn't been a meeting. There was nothing in the rules that said that everybody had to be there for a meeting. So, she would simply tell Stevie and Carole that the meeting had taken place without them and the rules had been voted into effect. Unanimously.

After all, that was true, wasn't it?

6

THE NEXT MORNING, Stevie slipped into the locker area of the tack room. She was really tired. After class yesterday, she'd spent about three hours trying to teach Nickel not to shy when he saw the Hula-Hoop twirl. The only thing she accomplished was getting him to shy as soon as he saw the thing, whether it was twirl- ing or not. A Hula-Hoop race was definitely out. To- day she'd try something with the baton from her closet. She couldn't think of any use for the broken umbrella.

She took off her sneakers and pulled on her riding boots. A lot of the time Stevie liked to ride in jeans and low boots, but in the summer, when she was spending five or six hours a day on horseback, breeches and high boots, though hotter, were a lot more com-

53

fortable. The high boots protected her legs from the straps and flaps on the saddle.

When her boots were on, she tried to shove her shoes and her boot hooks into her cubby, but there was something in it at the back, blocking the way. She leaned over to look into the knee-high nook. She couldn't see anything, but she also still couldn't fit her shoes in. It wasn't until she got down on her hands and knees and peered at the back of the cubby that she saw, crumpled and torn, the papers that Lisa had left for her the other day.

She reached in and pulled them out. At the top it read:

THE SADDLE CLUB
Rules

That was when Stevie remembered that Lisa's note called for a Saddle Club meeting at TD's. She'd gotten so busy with Nickel that she'd forgotten all about the meeting! She sat on the bench, staring at the papers. There was a dull, empty feeling in her stomach. She'd let her friends down.

Just then, Carole came into the locker area.

"Oh, Carole, I'm so sorry about yesterday," Stevie began, serious for once.

"What about yesterday?" Carole asked.

"The Club meeting at TD's . . ."

Carole looked blank for a second, then gasped. "Oh, no!" she said. "I forgot all about it. What happened?"

"I don't know," Stevie said. "That's what I'm sorry about. I wasn't there."

"You weren't? I wasn't either. I went over to the stable with Judy to check on that newborn foal. She was afraid the filly was getting sick, but it turned out she was okay. I looked for you to see if you wanted to come along, but I couldn't find you."

"Yeah, well, I was pretty busy too, planning the gymkhana, but that means we left Lisa out in the cold. Unless maybe she forgot, too."

"No way, considering how excited she was about those rules. Boy, I feel like a worm! Let's see if we can find her."

"Yeah, let's."

"Oh, Stevie!" It was Mrs. Reg, calling from her office off the tack room. "Come in here a moment, will you?"

"Sure, just a sec," Stevie called back. Then she turned to Carole. "Listen, you find Lisa and tell her how sorry we are. We can have a meeting at my house after drill practice this afternoon, okay? I've got to talk to Mrs. Reg. I'll see you both in class."

"I'll tell her, but I still feel like a worm."

"Well, she knows how busy we've both been—"

"Yeah, but still . . ."

"Stevie!" Mrs. Reg called.

"Coming."

Carole went in search of Lisa. Stevie stepped into Mrs. Reg's office and sat down on the tack box in front of her desk. "So, now, tell me," Mrs. Reg began. "How're you doing in making up games and races?"

That was another thing Stevie wasn't feeling too good about at the moment. So far, this day hadn't been exactly terrific. "To tell you the truth, Mrs. Reg, not so well. I've been trying to come up with some really original ideas. I spent a lot of time trying to make up a game with a Hula-Hoop, but that just spooked Nickel, and if he spooks, most of the other ponies will too. Then I tried a marshmallow game. No luck. I was sure I could get something going by riding on the saddle backward, but that only got Nickel confused—and me bruised! Finally, I've been working on something to do with Laser Tag. It's going to be wonderful, I'm sure, but the trouble is, I don't have a Laser Tag set to use yet. So, all in all, not so hot."

"How about an egg-and-spoon race?" Mrs. Reg asked brightly.

Stevie couldn't believe it. Every time she talked to someone about the gymkhana, all anybody ever suggested was an egg-and-spoon race. "Everybody already knows about egg-and-spoon races. I want to do something different, something interesting, something *fun*! Isn't that what Max wants, too?"

"Max wants a good set of games," Mrs. Reg said. "That doesn't necessarily mean they have to be so unusual that nobody can do them! Use your horse sense, Stevie," Mrs. Reg urged.

"Don't worry, Mrs. Reg," Stevie said. "I'm working on something with a baton that will be lots of fun. You'll see."

"Yes, I'm sure I will," Mrs. Reg said. "And I put a dozen eggs in the fridge if you want to give that a try, okay?"

Just then, the bell sounded. "Hey, class is about to start and I've still got to tack up Comanche. I'll talk to you next week again, Mrs. Reg."

"Okay," Mrs. Reg agreed. "By then, you should have a pretty good idea of the games you want to include, and you and I can start to plan a schedule and figure out how much time to allow and how to award points for prizes."

Schedule? Points? Prizes? How could they possibly do all that? Stevie had a growing awareness that she was going to have to move faster and work harder to make up the games if Mrs. Reg expected to plan a schedule and point system next week. That would mean another couple of hours on Nickel over the weekend. But how could she work harder than she was already working? It seemed impossible, for her and for Nickel.

Poor pony, she thought, sighing, as she headed for Comanche's stall with his tack. *Poor me*.

LISA ALMOST ALWAYS felt happy when she was riding. She'd gotten to like just about everything to do with it. She loved her clothes, the sleek breeches, the tall boots with the rich shine. She'd even gotten over being self-conscious about the hard hat they had to wear. She had only had to fall off once to appreciate how it could really be a lifesaver. When she'd first gotten her brand-new riding outfit, she'd thought it was silly and noticed how other people, even riders, stared at her. She knew now that was because everything had been so new that it sort of stuck out. Now her riding clothes showed wear—marks on her boots, smudges on her hat. *That* showed she was a real rider and she was proud of those marks and smudges.

Today, while the more advanced riders were in the jumping class, she was taking a "flat class." Estelle rode near her on a trail through some fields near Pine Hollow. Estelle's clothes were even newer than Lisa's. At first that seemed odd to Lisa, but she realized that Estelle must have bought new clothes in America. It would hardly be worth the trouble to bring a worn outfit all the way from France.

"How come you're not taking the jumping class?" Lisa asked. "I mean, you did jump, didn't you, on Napoleon?"

"Napoleon?" Estelle echoed. "Oh, right, well, I can't jump, see. My doctor won't let me do it."

"Why not? He must be a fuddy-duddy doctor if he won't let an experienced rider like you jump! I mean, Max says it's okay for us to start jumping as soon as we've been riding for a year. I just can't wait. I mean, I know he's right, but I'm ready, believe me!"

"I had an accident, you see," Estelle explained. "When I was a little girl, I hurt my back. I was in the hospital for a long time. I spent my seventh birthday in the hospital, it was horrible. The doctor said I should never jump. The risk is too great. So, here I am. Just happy to be able to ride at all."

"Oh, that's terrible. Does it still hurt?"

"My back? Oh, no, but, you see, it *could* hurt, and then I might not be able to ride ever again." Just then, Nero headed off the trail to the other side of the field at a trot. "*Arretez!*" Estelle yelled at him. "*À gauche! Maintenant! Cheval bête!*" Lisa had had enough French in school to know that Estelle was saying, "Stop! Turn left! Now! Stupid horse!"

Red O'Malley, who was instructing the class while Max worked with the jumpers, broke out of the file of riders and cantered over to rescue Estelle. All the riders watched in astonishment while Nero bolted, dumping Estelle unceremoniously in the grass. Within a few seconds, Red had recaptured the horse and led him back to Estelle. She stood in the middle of the field, brushing dirt and grass off her stylish riding breeches. Lisa suspected she was also rubbing something that was going to be a nasty bruise.

"Up you go," Red instructed her. Estelle just glared at the horse.

"I don't think I should have to ride him anymore," Estelle said. "He is too wild."

There were snorts of laughter from some of the riders. Everybody knew that Nero wasn't a wild horse. He was usually very complacent and gentle. Lisa couldn't understand why sweet old Nero was behaving so badly for Estelle.

"Estelle," Red said politely, "Nero just needs to have you let him know who is the boss. If he starts acting up, put more leg on him. It will remind him that you're on board and you're in charge. If that doesn't work, put some pressure on the reins. As a matter of fact, here, get up, and I'll show you what to do."

Reluctantly, Estelle remounted the horse. Red gave her the reins and explained that if she squeezed her fingers on the reins, alternating hands, it would put just the smallest amount of pressure on the bit in the horse's mouth. It wouldn't be enough pressure for him to think it was a signal, but it would be enough to make him think he should pay attention.

"Watch his ears when you do that," Red suggested. "You'll see that he's alert to *you* instead of doing his own thing."

When Estelle was back in the group they all started trotting. Lisa decided to try what Red had suggested, although her own horse, Pepper, hadn't been giving her any trouble. As soon as she squeezed the reins, moving them perhaps only a half an inch, Pepper seemed more alert to her, picked up his pace, and lifted his head sharply. It was a neat trick. Once she had his attention, she stopped doing it, but if he lagged, she could try it again.

Estelle, however, didn't seem to be having the same kind of luck. For the rest of the class she was fighting with Nero, and losing. Lisa thought it very strange indeed that Estelle should have such trouble. She'd never seen an experienced rider let her horse take the lead the way Nero did that day. Estelle must be right, she told herself. There was something terribly wrong with Nero.

When the class finally ended, Lisa got the soda whip. That was another one of Pine Hollow's traditions, and one that almost everybody enjoyed. Each class member pulled a riding whip out of a bucket. One of the whips had a bottle cap attached to it. It meant that rider was in charge of getting sodas for everybody in the class and delivering them to the stalls where the other students would be untacking their horses. Lisa took Pepper to his stall, then quickly scooped eight cans out of the little refrigerator in the tack room.

She delivered the drinks to the riders, ending with Estelle. When she opened Nero's stall, she found Estelle hanging onto the horse's bridle, almost being lifted off the ground by his nodding head. His ears were almost flat back against his head and his eyes were wide open, showing white. Lisa knew those were signs that the horse was very upset.

"Steady, boy," Lisa said, reaching to pat Nero's neck. "Take it easy, now. Nobody's going to hurt you. We just want to take off the bridle and saddle; calm down." He blinked his eyes and seemed to relax a little bit. "Let go of the bridle," Lisa told Estelle. Estelle released the bridle. The reins dangled to the ground. "Not the reins. Hold those!" Lisa told her sharply. It would be very easy for Nero to get his legs tangled in the long reins and then there would be *real* trouble.

Estelle's hand darted toward the reins, but when Nero tried to push her away with his nose, she jumped back, obviously scared. Lisa picked up the reins with her left hand and gave them to Estelle, who accepted them reluctantly.

"Whatsamatter, boy?" Lisa asked, still trying to calm the big horse. "We'll take care of you—no problem. Ready for some hay, maybe some fresh water?"

Lisa knew that the horse couldn't understand her. Max had told them all many times that horses couldn't speak English. But from experience, she also knew that horses could sense fear, and that they reacted with fear of their own. She tried to speak as calmly and fearlessly as possible. Finally, Nero got the message. His ears stood straight up, his head held steady, his liquid brown eyes gazed calmly at her.

Lisa continued to pat him while she removed his bridle. She handed it to Estelle and, with dismay, saw the French girl take it by one of the cheek straps. That was a sure way to tangle it, and Lisa would have to cope with that in a minute. First, though, she needed to finish with Nero. She loosened the girth and removed the saddle. The girls took the tack out of the stall, closed the door carefully, and carried the bridle and saddle back to the tack room.

"Come, help me with Pepper," Lisa said. "I'll show you what you need to do to keep a horse calm. Then we can give them both some water, okay?"

"I know how to take care of a horse!" Estelle snapped. "I have been doing it since I was a little girl!

Do you think I have really learned nothing in all these years? *I* do not need to learn anything. It is Nero who needs a lesson. Max must see to this right away." With that, Estelle turned and stormed off to Max's office.

Lisa was confused. Estelle was an experienced rider. She'd been riding for years. She owned her own horse. Still, she didn't seem to understand the simplest things about riding. It didn't make sense. Something didn't fit at all.

While she untacked Pepper and drank her own soda, Lisa thought about Estelle and the miserable day she had had with Nero. It was possible that Nero was ill. It was even possible that he needed to be taught a lesson, though if a rider felt a horse needed punishment of any kind, it was best to administer it at the very moment it was needed. What seemed the most possible, though, was that riding in France was very different from riding in America. Obviously, Estelle simply didn't know many of the things Lisa had been taught. Riders must be taught differently and horses must be trained differently in France, Lisa reasoned.

It was as if Estelle used a different language with her horse than Lisa did. Max often told his students that they spoke to their horses with their hands and their legs because a horse's sense of communication was more physical than anything. So, how could that be different in France? Lisa asked herself.

Once again, Lisa thought about the white stallion, Napoleon, a gift on Estelle's seventh birthday. Then Lisa recalled that Estelle had also told her that was a day she had spent in a hospital with a back injury. She must have heard it wrong—or else Estelle said it wrong.

When she'd stowed Pepper's tack, she brought him water and fresh hay and then did the same for Nero. By then he was completely calmed down, his same old placid self. He welcomed Lisa's pats and dug into the fresh hay enthusiastically.

Lisa shook her head in confusion. Something seemed out of kilter in her world, but she didn't know what it was.

Having no answer, and lost in thought, she slid his door shut and locked it.

7

"CAROLE, PAY ATTENTION!" Max snapped at Carole in jump class later that Friday. "If *you're* not paying attention, how can you expect your horse to do it?"

Carole tried again to focus. Diablo's ears perked up immediately in response to her soft tug on his reins. She circled the ring until he was in a nice, smooth, rocking canter, then she aimed him straight for the jump. It was a two-foot training jump, hardly a wall, but she knew that jumping high wasn't as important as jumping well. She approached the jump on Diablo, leaning forward ever so slightly, but holding the reins taut until they were close. Smoothly, she rose in the saddle and, keeping her back nearly parallel to the horse's neck, she leaned forward, letting the motion of

Diablo's head move her hands along his neck. Diablo lifted into the air and landed gently on the other side.

"See how well it works when you pay attention?" Max asked. Carole nodded her answer, but she hadn't really heard the question. Already her mind was someplace else. She was listening for the familiar sound of Judy's truck. The vet was due for Delilah's checkup and Carole hoped she'd arrive during the lunch break. Carole had noticed some changes in Delilah, and hoped that meant the foal's birth would be soon.

Something else distracted Carole as well. Lisa stood at the edge of the ring watching the end of the jump class. Carole hadn't had a chance to talk to her yet about missing yesterday's Club meeting. She knew how she'd feel if that had happened to her. She really wanted a chance to explain, but it seemed like every single second of the day was filled, at least up through their drill practice. And if Delilah was as close to her delivery as Carole suspected, she'd be even busier soon.

Just then, the French girl, Estelle, came into the ring and stood next to Lisa. Carole cringed. Estelle gave her goose bumps. Carole had watched her ride enough to know that she was a big phony on horseback—and probably everywhere else, too. When she'd overheard Estelle telling Meg Durham about this horse she'd supposedly been riding since she was seven, Carole had barely been able to contain her snort of laughter. There was no way Estelle had been riding for so long and learned so little! So what was she doing hanging around Lisa? Carole wondered.

AS SOON AS jump class was over, Stevie dashed into the tack room hoping to find Lisa there. There was no sign of her. Stevie took her sandwich and a soda from the refrigerator and went in search of her friend. Finally, in the stable area, she found a small crowd gathered near Delilah's stall. Lisa stood there along with seven or eight other students, watching Judy examine Delilah.

"Lisa, can I talk to you?" Stevie asked. Lisa turned in surprise. "I can't believe I forgot the meeting yesterday," Stevie rushed on. "I mean, I was busy with the gymkhana stuff, but that didn't mean I had to forget the Club meeting. I'm awfully sorry, especially since Carole told me she forgot, too. It was a terrible mistake, and I hope you can forget about it."

"It's okay, Stevie," Lisa said. "I just saw Carole, and she already told me how sorry you both were. It turned out all right anyway. Estelle was with me, so I wasn't hanging around there by myself, you know?"

Stevie felt an unbelievable rush of relief. From the second she'd realized what they'd done, she'd known how she would have felt if two friends had done that to her—and she knew that she wouldn't have been at all nice about it the way Lisa was being. Sighing happily, she slung her arm across Lisa's shoulder. "Thanks for understanding. How about a Club meeting at my house this afternoon after drill?"

"That'd be great," Lisa said.

"Now, what's going on here?" Stevie asked.

"Judy's examining Delilah. Carole's helping her."

Stevie stood on tiptoe to see. Carole was holding Delilah's halter while Judy felt around the horse's large belly. It was hard to believe, Stevie thought, that there really was another whole life growing inside the mare. And it wouldn't be long now before they'd all see it.

"Everything looks fine here," Judy said. Everybody seemed relieved, though there had never been any indication that anything was wrong. "And I still think we're on schedule for a delivery in a couple of weeks. This gal's not rushing into anything!" The girls all laughed. "But I'd better go now. I got a call on the way over here—"

"Judy!" Estelle called from the fringe of the group. "Before you go, could you take a look at Nero? He has been misbehaving terribly."

Judy glanced up at Estelle. "Old Nero? What's his trouble? Max didn't say anything to me—"

"Well, I didn't have time to tell him yet," Estelle explained.

"Sure, I'll look at him now," Judy agreed. "Describe his symptoms to me, will you?" While Judy packed her medical bag, Estelle explained the problems the horse had given her.

"Sounds like he's just cranky," Judy said.

"Le mot juste!" Estelle declared. Then she blushed, realizing nobody had understood her. "Excuse my French," she said. "It means that that is just exactly the right word."

Judy picked up her bag and followed Estelle to Nero's stall.

Stevie and a couple of the other girls tried to stifle giggles. They'd seen Estelle riding, and they knew it wasn't Nero who had the problem. *Le mot juste* was *phony*, Stevie thought.

Living near Washington meant that there were a lot of diplomats' children of all nationalities around. Stevie usually found them interesting and fun. Estelle was definitely an exception to that, though. Stevie didn't believe a word of her fantastic stories, and the idea that she'd been riding for a long time was just laughable.

Stevie looked for Lisa to continue their talk, but, much to her surprise, Lisa was following Estelle and Judy to Nero's stall.

Now, what's that about? Stevie asked herself. Shrugging for lack of an answer, Stevie headed for Nickel's stall. Carole was still busy with Delilah, and besides, she had a full hour at lunch to work on a game with a baton. A baton couldn't frighten a pony, could it?

"Hi, boy!" Stevie greeted Nickel cheerfully. Slowly, she pulled the baton out of her bag and showed it to the horse. Without hesitating, he reached for the white rubber tip of the baton and bit. Hard.

TWENTY MINUTES LATER, Lisa and Estelle sat together near the paddocks, eating their lunches.

"Gee, I'm glad to know Nero's okay," Lisa said. "When a horse gets sick, it can be big trouble, you know?"

"Of course I know," Estelle said quickly. "I have taken care of my horse when he was sick. Sometimes it's not pretty, either. Just last year, before the vet could treat him, he even threw up on me. It was awful, but he is my horse, you know, and I care for him like a child." Suddenly, Estelle changed the subject. "What was that you were talking with Stevie and Carole about?" she asked.

"Oh, they were explaining what happened yesterday, why they missed The Club meeting at TD's."

"Club? What is The Club?" Estelle asked.

Lisa had never spoken about the Club to anybody else. It wasn't exactly a secret. It just had always been more like a name for her friendship with Stevie and Carole, and until the rules had come along, that's really all it had been. Now Estelle wanted to know about it, and suddenly Lisa was terribly afraid Estelle would think it was silly.

"Well, we call it The Saddle Club," she explained. "It's sort of silly, I guess." That's all she could think to say.

"But what do you *do*?" Estelle asked insistently.

What did they do? Lisa asked herself. Until she'd written the rules she really would not have been able to answer that question, but now that there were rules,

70

and they had been passed—sort of—she could answer it—sort of.

"Well, we have meetings once a week or so, like yesterday afternoon, only since it was just me, it wasn't much of a meeting. But we plan projects, and help each other, and talk about horses, you know?"

"Oh, it sounds wonderful!" Estelle said. "You know, Lisa, it hasn't been easy for me, being new in America, to meet people and make friends. But a club like *that* . . . how many members are there in this club?"

"Well, just the three of us so far," Lisa told her.

"Three? Only three? Well, that's too bad, then," Estelle said.

Before Lisa could ask her why it was too bad, the bell sounded, signaling them to get ready for the next class. Estelle stood up quickly. "I must go see Max right away," she announced. "I will not ride Nero this afternoon. *Adieu.*" She walked off toward Max's office.

LATE THAT AFTERNOON, as soon as drill class was over, Lisa untacked Pepper, gave him something to eat and drink, and went in search of Stevie and Carole. Unlike the day before, she found them right away. Carole was already in Delilah's stall, carefully grooming her.

"Ready for the meeting?" Lisa asked.

"You bet," Carole said. "I still need to make up a batch of Delilah's special mash, but that'll just take me a few minutes. You and Stevie go on ahead. Don't wait for me. I'll join you at Stevie's, okay?"

"Sure," Lisa agreed. "Know where Stevie is?"

"I think she's having a serious talk with Nickel. She can't get that poor pony to do anything she wants him to."

"I'll go cheer her on," Lisa said. "See you in a little while." Lisa jogged over to Nickel's stall. There she saw Stevie holding a mangled drum majorette's baton.

"What's that for?" she asked.

"Depends on your point of view," Stevie said. "Nickel, for instance, thinks it's dinner, since he already had a piece of it for lunch."

Stevie looked so serious that Lisa couldn't help laughing. "You're funny, you know that?"

"Boy, I wish it were funny," Stevie said. "This old guy is supposed to be the backbone of the pony-game team, and I'm having a heck of a time convincing him to have any fun."

"If anybody can do it, you can," Lisa said encouragingly. "And speaking of having some fun, Carole said we should go along to your house ahead of her. She has to make the special mash for Delilah and will be a couple of minutes late."

"You all ready to go now?" Stevie asked.

"Yup."

"I've got to finish up here first. It'll be about ten minutes. I'll meet you in the tack room, okay?"

Lisa had an idea. "Since you and Carole are each working on something for a few minutes, I think I'll go on ahead. I've got an errand to run at the shopping center. It'll only take me about twenty minutes. I can meet you at your house because it's practically on the way. Okay?"

"Sounds fine to me. If you get there first, get my mom to show you where the chocolate chip cookies are, okay?"

"Deal," Lisa said.

FIFTEEN MINUTES LATER, Lisa was back in the jewelry store at the shopping center, once again looking in the case where the horse-head pin was kept. In her pocket was the birthday cash she'd gotten from her mother's sister. Aunt Elizabeth, after whom she'd been named, was her godmother, too, and a pretty generous one at that. Lisa hoped the money she had would be enough to buy a pin for every member of The Saddle Club. Maybe even more than rules, that would make it a *real* club.

"CAROLE, THAT DOESN'T look right," Max said. "Are you sure you followed the recipe that Judy gave you for Delilah's bran mash?"

"I think so, Max. Look, here, I put a scoop of concentrated grain into the boiling water, then four scoops of wheat bran—"

"No, no, that's not a one—that's a four. You have to start with four scoops of grain. You're going to have to throw this out and start again."

"But *Max*!" Carole said in exasperation.

"You wanted to know how to take care of a mare, Carole," he reminded her.

"Yes, Max," she said, dumping her mistake into the garbage. It wouldn't be at all fair to Delilah to give her a mistake when she and her foal needed wholesome, nourishing food. "But I'm supposed to be somewhere now. Can I use the phone?"

Like all good stables, Pine Hollow had phones near the stalls so someone taking care of a horse wouldn't have to leave it alone to summon help. It was a special privilege to make a call from the stable. Max agreed.

Carole thought it was odd that Stevie and Lisa hadn't gotten to Stevie's when she called, but she left the message with Stevie's brother Chad. He promised to tell Stevie and Lisa that she just couldn't make it.

"NICKEL? NICKEL? YOU didn't really swallow that, did you? Nickel?"

Stevie glared at the pony and he glared back at her dully. He swished his tail uneasily and then stomped at the floor repeatedly. She didn't like the way he was behaving. She'd seen horses with colic before and Nickel was showing signs of it. A colicky horse was one with a digestive problem, a stomachache, but in a horse it could be a very serious problem—especially when it might have been caused by the horse eating something like the rubber end of a baton!

Stevie slipped her fingers into Nickel's mouth and twisted them to make him open up. He didn't like that at all. Nickel pulled away and tried to nip at her.

There was no way she'd be able to see if the rubber was still in his mouth. This was going to take an expert, maybe even a vet. How on earth was she going to explain to Max or Judy how Nickel had eaten a piece of rubber?

But his health was a lot more important than her embarrassment. Stevie secured his stall and went into Max's office. She *had* to tell him what she'd done. He listened carefully while Stevie described Nickel's symptoms and he waited while she explained what might have caused it.

"I'm not sure, Max. I didn't actually see him swallow it. But it could be in him now."

"No time to waste," Max said. "I'll go to Nickel. You call Judy and tell her to get here right away. We'll talk about how it happened later."

Her heart thumping with worry about Nickel, Stevie sat down at the phone at Max's desk and dialed Judy's number. She was so relieved when Judy answered it herself, and even more relieved when Judy told Stevie she was only about five minutes away. She'd be right there.

Before returning to Nickel's stall, Stevie made one more call. She knew Carole and Lisa would understand. She had to stay with Nickel until he was better. It was her responsibility.

"Oh, Chad?" she said when her brother answered the phone. "Listen, I'm in a rush. There's an emergency here at the stable. Tell Carole and Lisa that Nickel's sick and I've got to stay here. I don't know when I'll be home. I'm sorry, but they'll understand. Bye."

She hung up quickly and headed back to Nickel's stall.

LISA WALKED HAPPILY up the stone stairs that led to Stevie's front door and rang the bell. She'd been able to buy four pins with her birthday money. There would be one for each member of The Saddle Club and one for the first new member they voted into the Club. And Lisa knew just who she thought that should be.

Chad Lake opened the door. "Hi there, uh, Lisa. Come on in."

"Carole and Stevie here yet?" she asked, stepping through the doorway.

"Well, not exactly," Chad began uncomfortably. "Both of them called. I mean each of them called. But they didn't know that the other wasn't coming. Say, why don't you come in anyway? I mean, I'm sure Stevie would want you to come in and anyway, if it had been me, I wouldn't have missed a meeting with you." He grinned warmly at her. Lisa was a little surprised by the way he was acting toward her, but she was more surprised by what her friends had done. Even from Chad's slightly garbled message, it was clear that neither Stevie nor Carole was going to be able to make it to *this* meeting either.

Furious, and shrugging off Chad's offer of cookies, milk, or video games, she stomped back down the stairs, shoving The Club pins deep into her pants pocket.

"They'll see," she muttered to herself as she turned toward home. "They'll see."

She barely got the door to her own room closed before the hot tears began streaming down her cheeks.

What had happened to The Saddle Club?

NOBODY EVER SAID Lisa Atwood wasn't resourceful. She always managed to find a way to accomplish things—even when they seemed impossible. Lisa knew this about herself, but she was beginning to think that The Saddle Club would be her greatest challenge.

She stopped crying after a few minutes. Then she sat sullenly on her bed, glaring out at space. She could have gone on doing that for a while, but Dolly scratched at her door. One look at that cute little face with its golden fur, and she couldn't help smiling a little.

She'd worked for hours and hours on the rules for the Club, just to make it a *real* club. Now that she'd accomplished that, it was beginning to look as if it didn't matter to Carole and Stevie what she did. In her orderly mind, the possibilities began slipping into place. If Carole and Stevie wanted out of the Club, she couldn't stop them, and if they left, one of two things would happen: The Club would stop altogether, or—or it would continue only if there were other members.

That had to be the answer. Lisa pulled the set of rules out of her desk drawer. Right there, Rule Four in the New Members section said that new members could be voted in at any Club meeting by a majority of the members present. Well, there *was* a Club meeting, right? Just because Carole and Stevie hadn't shown up didn't mean it wasn't a Club meeting.

Lisa decided it was time for formalities. "I'd like to propose a new member for The Saddle Club," she said. Dolly's ears perked up. She lifted her head from her paws and looked at Lisa. "I'd like to propose that we admit Estelle Duval." Dolly put her head back down on her paws. "Is there any discussion?" Dolly blinked her eyes. "Shall we vote?" Lisa asked. "All in favor say 'aye.'" She waited a few seconds and then voted in favor of Estelle's admission to The Saddle Club. "All opposed?" There was no opposition. "Well, then, it's settled," Lisa told Dolly. "We now have four members in The Saddle Club."

She took out the four small pins she'd bought that afternoon and laid them in a line on her bed. She loved the regal horse head with his mane swept back by the wind. She'd be proud to wear her pin, symbol of both her friendship and her love of horses. She picked up the first pin and stepped over to her mirror. Carefully, she unlocked the clasp and slid the pin through the fabric of her blouse. There was a little fingerprint on the horse's head. She took a tissue and wiped the pin until it gleamed.

"Lisa, phone for you," her mother called up the stairs.

Lisa opened her door. "Who is it?" she asked.

"Stevie."

"Tell her I'm busy," Lisa said, and when her mother looked a little bit shocked, she added, "Please."

"Sure, hon," Mrs. Atwood agreed. "I'll tell her."

A few minutes later, there was a call from Carole. Lisa didn't speak to her either. She just wasn't in the mood to hear their excuses.

There was also a little corner of her that knew she wasn't quite ready to tell her friends about the things that had gone on at the Club meetings they'd missed.

They'd find out in time—and it would serve them right for not paying any attention to anything she was doing.

STEVIE HUNG UP the phone in a fury. Trying to talk the Zieglers into letting her borrow their Laser Tag had been a lousy idea. Absolutely nothing was working out. Well, that wasn't quite true, she reminded herself. After all, right after Judy had arrived to examine Nickel, Stevie had found the missing chunk of rubber from the baton. It had landed in the peat and straw on the floor of his stall. It had never gotten anywhere near his stomach. Nickel got a clean bill of health from Judy, and Stevie got a well-deserved lecture about horse care from Max.

What really made her angry, though, was that she'd spent more than a week trying to create new and interesting games and races for the gymkhana and she'd gotten nowhere at all. It certainly wasn't her fault, though. She'd done everything she could and nothing had worked. Now Max was angry with her, Mrs. Reg was worried that they wouldn't have any games for the young riders, Carole was too busy with Delilah to talk to her, and Lisa spent all her time with Estelle Duval. She wasn't getting help from anybody. Even her very own twin brother, Alex, had refused to help her with the Laser Tag game.

The crowning glory had come that evening at the dinner table when she'd told her family how much trouble she was having with the games. She was admitting nearly total defeat by announcing it at dinner.

"I've got an idea for a neat relay race," her father had said. "I'm pretty sure you can do it on horseback."

"What is it, Dad?" she'd asked excitedly.

"Well, it's kind of a spoon race, but, you know, carrying eggs?"

Why in the world couldn't anybody suggest something that didn't have to do with eggs?

CAROLE SLID WEARILY into the overstuffed chair in the living room, where her father sat polishing his shoes. Next in line was the brass.

"Inspection tomorrow, huh?" Carole asked.

"Yes, and if there's one thing I've learned it's that the colonel's leather and brass have to be brighter and shinier than the troops'."

"Let me do the shoes, Dad. I get so much experience at the stable with saddles and bridles that I can always make leather shine. Besides, you'll never get a shine unless it's really clean. Don't you have any saddle soap?"

"At my age—and with eighteen years in the Marine Corps—I'm getting polishing lessons from a twelve-year-old?" He laughed. "You're welcome to them." He handed Carole his shoes and belt.

Carole brought a tin of saddle soap into the living room from her room, took her father's shoes, and began cleaning them thoroughly.

"What's got you so droopy these days, hon? I thought you were excited about that mare. Isn't she going to foal any day now?"

"That's what Judy says. But it's so much work, Dad. You know Delilah has to have a special bran mash, and it's a real nuisance to make. I had to make three batches tonight before I got it right. Then I had to wait for it to cool before I could give it to her. Imagine, cooking for a horse! I thought it would take me just ten minutes, but it took me hours. It's not that I don't care about Delilah, I do. Really. But it's a *lot* of work."

"Don't your friends help you with that kind of thing?"

"I sort of expected that they would, but they're so busy with their own things . . ."

The colonel applied a small smear of brass polish to his belt buckle and began rubbing vigorously. "Sounds to me like you're too busy to help them with their projects, too, aren't you?"

"Well, yeah," Carole admitted. "Do you know that I have to clean Delilah's stable twice as often now that she's almost due? Judy says it's terribly dangerous to have a foal born in an unsanitary stall. And with all the hay she's eating these days—"

"Spare me the details," her father said, laughing. Carole grinned. She'd finished cleaning the first shoe. She picked up the second. "Oh, wait'll I tell you what General Morris's aide did today," the colonel said, chatting about his day. Carole listened, applying polish to the shoes and buffing hard until each had a deep shine.

Carole displayed the gleaming shoes proudly when he'd finished talking. "See how shiny you can get them when you use saddle soap before you polish them?"

"Hey, that's great," her father said, admiring the shine on his shoes. "So we've gotten some benefit from your horseback riding after all. Very good. And look at me. I'm all done with my brass, too. Work always goes faster and better when two people do it at once. At least, that's what I think."

"You know, I think you're right," Carole mused. Then the truth finally occurred to her. "And I think it goes even faster and better when *three* people do it at once."

"Interesting idea," her father said. "I've got to hit the rack now. Inspection's very early."

"Me too. Judy's coming to check Delilah early tomorrow, so even though it's Saturday, you can still drop me off at Pine Hollow."

"Good night, Carole."

"Night, Dad," she said, giving him the great big hug he deserved. "You're the greatest."

9

FIRST THING MONDAY morning, Carole wanted to talk to Stevie and Lisa. The talk she'd had with her father had made her understand a lot of things—first and foremost that she and her friends really needed one another. She got to the stable especially early to allow extra time, but she'd forgotten that Stevie and Lisa couldn't have known she wanted to see them. She was just pulling on her second boot when Judy's truck drove up in front of the stable. She waved at the vet through the dirty window and met her in Delilah's stall. She'd talk to her friends later, she decided.

Stevie dashed into the locker area a half hour before class started. She needed every spare moment these days. She finished dressing in a matter of minutes, then started looking for some gear for the gymkhana in the tack box outside Mrs. Reg's office.

When Lisa arrived at the stable fifteen minutes before class, she wasn't surprised to see both of her friends totally occupied. As usual, Carole was with Judy in Delilah's stall. Stevie was shuffling through boxes of stuff in the tack room. It wasn't clear what she wanted, but it was clear she wasn't finding it. Lisa left her alone.

Once she'd donned her riding clothes, Lisa sat on the fence in front of the stable, waiting for The Saddle Club's newest member. Estelle usually arrived at the last minute, so Lisa wasn't going to have much time. What she had to say would only take a moment, but it should be fun. It was always nice to share good news.

Lisa was wearing her own Saddle Club pin. She knew it was just a pin, although in her opinion, it was a very pretty pin. What was important to her—even more important than the pin itself—was what the pin represented. It told her, and the people who mattered to her, that she cared deeply about horses—that she loved them and could ride them and that, after her friends, horses were about the most important thing in the world to her. She was sure the sun gleaming off the shiny surface of her horse-head pin made it even more beautiful.

Just then, Estelle's chauffered Citroën pulled into the drive. The rear door opened slowly and Estelle emerged sedately. That was an interesting thing about Estelle, Lisa thought as she waited for her. There were only about three minutes until class. If *she* were that late, she'd be running at full speed. Estelle, however, never seemed to be in a hurry. As a result, Max was forever speaking to her about keeping other people (especially him) waiting. That didn't speed her up, though.

"Hi, Estelle," Lisa said brightly, falling in step with the French girl.

"Oh, good morning, Lisa," she replied, walking toward the stable.

"I've got some good news for you," Lisa said, hoping she sounded as cool and sophisticated as Estelle always did.

"Yes?"

"It's about The Saddle Club," Lisa said. "There was a meeting Friday night and you were voted in."

"Voted in?" Estelle repeated. "What does this mean?"

"It means you're now a member of The Saddle Club," Lisa told her, grinning proudly. "And as a member, you're entitled to wear our pin."

"Oh?"

Lisa was pleased by Estelle's obvious interest and she handed Estelle her pin. It was wrapped in tissue so it wouldn't get any fingerprints on it.

Estelle carefully unwrapped the tissue and then held the pin in her hand for a moment. "It's a horse head," she said flatly.

"Yes, and isn't it pretty? See how nice and shiny it is? We can all wear our pins on our jackets and that can show other riders that we're all friends. Here, I'll help you pin it on," Lisa offered.

"Thanks, but I can put it on myself," Estelle said. "I'll do it later. I'm late now." For once, Estelle seemed to be in a hurry. She shoved the pin in her pocket, letting the tissue fall onto the ground. "See you in class," she told Lisa, turning to the stable.

Lisa was too stunned to move. Could she be mistaken? Lisa was trying to share one of the most important things in her life with her new friend, and unless she was totally off her mark, Estelle wasn't in the least bit excited, either about the Club *or* about the beautiful pin. How could that be?

It just wasn't possible, Lisa decided. Estelle really *was* in a hurry. She'd probably have her pin on in time for class.

Once Lisa had given Estelle the pin, she felt very relieved. The deed was done. If Stevie and Carole didn't like it, that was their problem. They should have come to the meetings.

MAX WAS IN an especially strict mood that day. He had all of his students working harder than ever before. There was no fooling around at all, all day long.

"Boy, if he tells me to keep my heels down one more time, I'm going to scream," Lisa confided to Carole during the chore period. Lisa had hoped to be assigned to do something with Estelle so they could talk about the Club some more, but Estelle and Veronica were tending to the horses in the paddocks. As it turned out, Lisa, Carole, and Stevie were all assigned to cleaning tack.

"He's got a thing about heels today, that's for sure," Carole agreed, "and toes. I found myself forcing mine inward every time he was facing me!"

"*That* must be why I heard him tell you not to stick your heels out!"

"Just my luck," Carole said. "I hope he'll go a little easier during jump class."

"You always do well then, don't you?"

"Not always," Carole said.

"I wish you could be in jump class too, Lisa," Stevie said.

"Me too. I like riding on the trail, but the only students there are the babies, except for me and Estelle." Carole and Stevie exchanged glances. "Red is so worried that somebody's going to get hurt that he'll barely let us trot. You'd think he'd let us do something more daring, like cantering, more often," Lisa said.

"Well, you certainly can," Stevie began. "I don't know about Estelle, though. She seems pretty green to me."

"Oh, no," Lisa said. "She's been riding for years—since she was five."

"She has?"

"Yes, and she has her own horse and her family has this country home with a stable near Paris where they go on weekends. They're all just as horse crazy as we are. But they do things differently in France, that's all.

She has to get used to the American way of doing things."

"Girls," Mrs. Reg called from her office. "Not so much gabbing, please. There's a lot of work to be done today. All of the dressage saddles are positively dingy and we'll need them for the upcoming show. Now, see if you can finish those before your next class."

"I think it's running in the family today," Stevie whispered. The three girls burst into giggles—and then muffled them right away so Mrs. Reg wouldn't hear.

"You still talking in there?" she called out.

"No ma'am," Carole said politely. "We're not talking anymore."

"Right, we're just giggling," Stevie whispered to her friends. "That's more fun anyway."

"Which are the dressage saddles?" Lisa asked.

"Those over there," Carole said, pointing to ten saddles stored together. "See how the flap is straight on both sides and how the rider will sit back in the saddle? It gives the rider more control over the horse. Wait'll you see. When dressage is done right, it's fantastic."

"Girls!"

Lisa hung up the bridle she'd been working on and brought one of the dressage saddles over to clean. They'd each have to do three, and then whoever finished first could do the last one while the other two cleaned up. It wouldn't be so bad if they worked together, she thought.

AT THREE O'CLOCK, Stevie, Lisa, and Carole were all together again, this time for drill practice. Normally, Stevie wasn't particularly interested in things that required such precision. Her whole personality was more flamboyant. But this drill work was just plain fun as far as she was concerned.

"What we're working on now is something I call the clover leaf," Max explained. "Normally, it's a four-leaf clover, but with just three of you, a three-leafer is better. But harder."

With that, he explained how each rider was to lead off on her own "leaf" in a clockwise path, leading into the next rider's leaf.

"The whole pleasure here for the audience is seeing how you *don't* run into each other at the cross. Try it."

Carole led off on the bottom right leaf. Stevie followed, two trotting paces later, on the upright leaf. Lisa went last, two paces after Stevie. Somehow, magically, when it came to the cross, Carole passed through first, then Stevie, then Lisa.

"Wonderful, girls! That was *great*. I've seen so-called experts who couldn't manage that maneuver anywhere near as well as you can. You three work together *so* well! Now, try it again, but keep it going as long as you can."

It turned out that "as long as you can" was only three times through the exercise. By then, Carole was well ahead of the other riders, and Lisa and Stevie were practically ramming into each other at the cross.

"It's still good," Max told them. "At least you could get through it enough times so each of you could complete the clover. You should be proud of what you can do together."

Stevie was beaming with the pleasure of success, and one glance at her friends confirmed that they were feeling the same way. But was this really *Max* talking?

"What I want you to do next is to begin trotting at the edge of the ring, evenly spaced and proceeding in a circle. As I instruct you, make your circle smaller, but maintaining a uniform distance from one another. At the end, you should have your horses practically head-to-tail, at the same speed, in a very small circle at the center of the ring. Think you can do it?"

At that moment, Stevie thought they could do anything. The three girls brought their horses to a nice collected trot, as close to the pace of the horse in front as they could. Then Max had them begin the exercise.

It turned out to be much trickier than Stevie expected. If horses follow one another, they always seem to want to catch up to the horse in front. Horses are naturally competitive, and one of the ways they prove that is by racing—even when they're not supposed to, like in a drill exercise. No matter how hard Stevie tried, it seemed almost impossible to control Comanche's trot. And as soon as Comanche quickened his pace to catch up with Diablo, Pepper wanted to get into the act. Pretty soon, all three horses were trotting contentedly on one side of the ring. The girls tried it four times and each time the same thing happened.

"I think there's some work to be done here, girls," Max said. "You should have better control of your horses, you know. Perhaps we should try again next time."

"Can't we try again now?" Stevie asked.

"Not now, Stevie. I've got a private lesson to give on the trail and it's time for you all to go home now."

"One more time?" Lisa asked.

"As I said, I have to go. If you all want to work on it by yourselves, of course, you may, but only for a few minutes. The horses need a rest, too. Good night," he said. Then, as only Max could, he bowed to his students and left the ring.

"We can do better," Stevie said.

"You bet we can," Lisa agreed. "I mean, I know that clover thing was harder than this, but it seems almost impossible to keep Pepper from running up to Diablo."

"Music," Carole said suddenly. "I think that's the answer."

"Hey, great idea!" Stevie said.

"The horses can follow the beat of the music?" Lisa said in wonderment.

"I doubt it," Carole told her, "but *we* can. See, then we can maintain an even beat with our posting. If we're all going up-down at the same beat, we can use that to guide our horses to the pace we want."

"Well, we'll work this out together, won't we?" Stevie asked. The grins on her friends' faces answered the question.

"I'll go see what tapes Mrs. Reg has that she can put on the P.A. system for us, okay? Here, hold Diablo for me, will you?"

Stevie took the reins from Carole and watched while she dashed off to Mrs. Reg's office.

CAROLE WAS NEARLY breathless with excitement. She loved the drill work as much as her friends did and she was thrilled to have come up with a possible solution to a big problem.

Mrs. Reg wasn't in her office, though, and Carole suddenly remembered that she had scheduled a trip to the saddle shop for supplies for the horse show. The office was completely locked up, so although the music idea was a good one, they couldn't try it today.

Disappointed, Carole headed back to the outdoor ring. The stable was quiet. Max was on the trail with his private student; Mrs. Reg was at the shop; and except for the three of them, the camp class had all gone for the day. Even Red O'Malley was away. He'd gone along with Mrs. Reg.

Carole glanced at the horses' stalls as she passed, clucking gently, patting noses here and there, feeling very much in charge, and liking it.

She detoured around to say hello to Delilah, isolated in her foaling stall. Usually Delilah had her head out over the top of the sliding door, but there was no sign of her today.

Curious, Carole clucked, but there was no response, no familiar nodding head with its platinum forelock.

She clucked again. This time she heard a mild whinny. Carole hastened to the door of the special stall. When she looked in, what she saw made her heart jump.

Delilah was in a far corner of the stall. She was pacing back and forth, alternately pawing at the ground and kicking at her own belly. Her tail switched rapidly, flicking upward as well as sideways. There was a froth of sweat on her flanks and her chest.

There was no doubt about it. Delilah was in labor. Her foal was about to be born—and the only people in the stable were Carole, Stevie, and Lisa!

10

WITHIN SECONDS, CAROLE marshaled her troops. "Stevie, you call Judy. Tell her I'm just about certain Delilah's in labor, and find out how long it'll take her to get here. Lisa, put the horses in their stalls and untack them. Then both of you come on back to Delilah's stall. There's work to be done!"

Carole pivoted on her toes and raced back to Delilah, excited, nervous, relieved that the time had come, really come. The mare was still storming back and forth in the stall when Carole got back. Hoping to calm her, Carole reached over the tall door and tried to pat Delilah soothingly. Delilah swept her head back, obviously rejecting the affectionate pat. Once again, the horse appeared to be kicking at her belly, and then she began digging away at the clean hay in her stall, almost as if she were making a nest.

"Judy'll get here as soon as she can," Stevie reported, approaching the stall cautiously. "Her assistant told me a horse over at Ridge Farm got attacked by a group of dogs and needs a zillion stitches. She really can't leave now. It'll be at least an hour before she's done and then a half hour to get here. She won't have the foal that fast, will she?" Stevie asked.

"No way to tell," Carole said calmly. "This is Delilah's first foal. It could be a few minutes. It could be a day or more. To tell you the truth, I know she's showing early symptoms of being in labor, but I have no idea how long these last." Carole glanced at the horse and her calm quickly vanished. "Oh, no!"

"What's the matter?"

"Look at her udder," Carole said. "See the milk coming out of it? I'm sure Judy told me that meant things were moving rapidly—or did she say it was something that could happen a lot before the foal arrives? I don't know—I don't remember!" she said, nearly frantic.

"Hey, hey, calm down," Stevie said. "We're all here, and we're going to help you *and* Delilah. It's going to be okay. This horse is going to have the most beautiful foal ever born, and we'll see to it that it happens right. Besides, if I remember correctly, horses have been having baby horses a lot longer than people have been trying to help them. Isn't Delilah going to do most of the work, anyway?"

"Yeah, I guess so," Carole said, smiling bashfully. "I just care so much about this foal, and its mother—"

"And its father, right?" Stevie asked softly, reminding Carole of Cobalt, the coal-black Thoroughbred who had sired the foal. "We won't let him down, either, will we?"

"Yeah, right. I just don't want to let how much I care make me nervous."

"Nervous? Who's nervous?" Lisa asked, arriving all out of breath.

"Me," Carole confessed.

"No need to be nervous," Lisa said reassuringly. "Stevie and I are right here beside you, ready to do your bidding. What's the first thing we do?"

All of a sudden, Carole's mind was a complete blank. She couldn't remember anything Judy had ever told her about *anything*, much less about foaling. Delilah's insistent stomping only made her more confused. She felt tense knowing she would be practically useless to Delilah just when the mare needed her the very most. But without her help, would the foal make it? Carole could barely speak.

"The birthing kit—where is it?" Stevie asked, breaking through Carole's terror.

"Oh, yes, that's right. We need that. It's in the chest, right over there."

Stevie turned and opened the chest where Carole and Judy had only recently stowed the birthing kit. It was really just a cardboard carton, but it contained all the things an owner routinely needed to assist at a normal delivery. Everything was carefully arranged in the order in which it was most likely to be needed. Right on top was a big roll of three-inch gauze bandage.

That made it all come back to Carole. "I remember now. Thanks for reminding me about the birthing kit, Stevie. For a moment there, I couldn't have told you my name, much less what we'd have to do for Delilah. First thing, though, grab that roll of gauze, okay? We have to bind up Delilah's tail. I'll hold her head and see if I can keep her relatively calm and distracted while you wrap her tail. See, we don't want those long hairs to get in the way of anything or to carry any germs that could cause infections. She's better off if we just fold it up and wrap it up."

Cautiously, the two of them entered Delilah's stall. The horse eyed her visitors uncertainly. Carole grasped the mare's halter gently and began rubbing her nose and forehead. The familiar affectionate motion seemed to calm the horse.

"There, there, girl. We'll take care of you," Carole said soothingly.

"I never wrapped a tail before," Stevie said from the horse's rear. "But my mother says I'm the best in the house at Christmas presents. My biggest challenge was an umbrella. Did you ever try to wrap something so it didn't look like what's actually in the package?"

"I don't think Delilah's going to mind if her tail ac-tually *looks* like a tail," Carole teased.

"No problem," Stevie said cheerfully, rolling the gauze carefully around the folded tail. "It's still going to look like a tail, just a well-wrapped one. There, I think that will do it. Scissors please, Lisa."

Lisa passed the scissors over. Stevie finished up her task with a flourish. "Ta-*da*!" she said.

Carole had to admit she'd never seen a more nicely wrapped tail, nor one with a prettier bow on it! "I'm sure Delilah will appreciate that," Carole said. "Okay, next, she needs to be cleansed with a disinfectant. Your turn, Lisa."

Following Carole's instructions, Lisa used the cleansing soap and disinfectant on Delilah's hindquarters. With Carole continuing her sweet talk to Delilah, the horse seemed to be almost unaware of what Lisa was doing.

"Finished," Lisa announced. "She's as clean as I can make her."

"That's great. Now come on out of the stall. I'm going to follow you. We should move carefully so as not to upset Delilah, okay?"

Smoothly and quietly the girls left Delilah alone in her stall. Carole slid the door closed and latched it.

"Well, look at Delilah," Stevie teased. "She's all squeaky clean and purtied up. What comes next?"

"We wait," Carole said. "And that's probably all we can do—that is if Delilah does what she's supposed to do. . . ."

"And where do we wait?"

"We wait where she can't see us. Judy says that mares don't like to be watched—"

"We can't *watch*? I thought that was what we've been waiting to do," Stevie complained.

"Oh, we can watch, all right. I wouldn't miss it for the world. We just can't watch where she can see us, or at least not where she's aware of us. We can hide right here in the next stall. We need to be pretty quiet, but we can see everything right through the knotholes."

"Don't tell me Delilah doesn't know we're here," Lisa said as they made their way into the empty stall.

"Oh, if she thought about it, she would," Carole said. "But Delilah's got other things on her mind right now. As long as we stay pretty much out of sight, we'll be out of mind."

"How long is this going to take?" Lisa asked.

"Psst! Delilah's lying down!" Stevie said, looking through the hole.

"What does that mean?" Lisa asked.

"It means she's tired," Carole explained.

"She's standing up again!" Stevie reported.

"What does *that* mean?" Lisa asked.

"It means she's had enough rest," Carole told her.

"She's pawing at the straw again," Stevie said.

"What does that mean?" Lisa asked.

"It means she's trying to build a sand castle, right, Carole?" Stevie joked.

"Whatever you say, Stevie," Carole said, laughing.

"I'm hungry," Stevie said a moment later.

"Well, I've got some good things to eat here," Carole said. "I put my cot and all my snacks in this stall so

I could stay here while I waited for Delilah to foal. Now it sort of looks like I won't need all that food, because something tells me Delilah isn't going to take all that long. Here." Carole reached for a large backpack. She unzipped it and began producing the goodies she'd expected to eat alone.

"I never saw such a lot of nourishing food all at once," Stevie joked, looking over the array of cupcakes, cookies, candy bars, and chips.

"Food from all the major food groups, I see," Lisa quipped.

"Yeah, the cupcake-and-cookie group, the peanut-and-popcorn group, the chips-and-crackers group, the—"

"You want it or don't you?" Carole asked.

"You bet I want it," Stevie said.

"Me too," Lisa agreed, reaching for the bag of cookies. "I usually have a snack when I get home in the afternoon and I'm usually home much earlier than this. No wonder I'm so hungry—yeah, what time is it, anyway?"

Stevie glanced at her watch. "Five-fifteen! My mother's going to be worried. I'd better give her a call."

"We all better call home," Lisa agreed.

Temporarily abandoning their snack, the girls headed for the phone and hurriedly made their calls. Stevie's mother agreed to pick up all of them when they were ready to leave. Another round of calls resolved that, and the girls returned to the empty stall next to Delilah's.

"Something's different," Stevie reported from her vantage point at the largest knothole.

"What do you mean?" Carole asked.

"Well, for one thing, Delilah's lying down, but not on her stomach. She's lying on her side, and her legs are sticking straight out. She looks weird and uncomfortable. Is she okay?" Carole was upset by the worry in Stevie's voice.

"Let me see!" Carole got onto her knees and peered through the hole. There was Delilah, just like Stevie said, lying on her side. But Stevie had forgotten to mention a few things. "She isn't just lying there—she's having contractions! See her muscles rippling? And unless I miss my guess by a mile, I can see the foal's feet! The baby's coming and it's coming *now!*"

All three girls got to their feet and climbed up on the horizontal slats that separated the two stalls. About six feet up, the wood stopped and there was only a screen. They could see more clearly there because they could see the whole stall at once.

"Look, there it is, don't you see? The little feet, now there are two of them. The foal is still in the sack—that's the white part—but you can see the outline of its pointy little hooves, and now—look, the foal's nose!"

All three girls gasped in awe at the foal's emergence. Nothing that had ever happened to any of them before could prepare them for the event that was taking place then.

"You know, I always knew in a sort of textbook way that there was a foal inside that mare, but to see it, to actually *see* it. That's not like a textbook at all. I mean—that's real," Lisa said. "And it's incredible."

"You got that right," Stevie agreed.

"Come on, girls," Carole said. "Delilah needs our help now. Where's the birthing kit?"

"Right here," Lisa announced. "What do you need?"

"I need the scissors. Judy told me how to do this when the other foal was born. I'm pretty sure I know what to do. See, we need to cut the sack—"

Just then, Delilah had another contraction and more of the foal emerged, and before Carole could enter the stall and cut the sack, there was a final contraction and the foal was completely born. Then the sack broke open by itself. The little baby lifted its head and looked at the world around it, sniffing tentatively. Delilah looked warily at her foal, then nudged the baby with her nose, sniffing, too.

"They're getting acquainted," Carole explained. "Aren't they adorable?"

Lisa and Stevie nodded, not wanting to take their eyes off the foal.

"What color is it?" Stevie asked.

"Hard to tell when it's so wet," Lisa added.

"It's black," Carole said in a daze. "Coal-black, just like its father—just like I knew it would be."

"Look!" Lisa said. "It's trying to stand up."

The foal moved its front legs forward, awkwardly pushing from the rear. It didn't work, though. As soon as its rear legs began to straighten, its front legs collapsed, sending the newborn sprawling into the straw bedding.

The girls burst into laughter.

Delilah, having rested for a few minutes, stood up and regarded her baby, sniffing it all over, looking at it from all directions. Apparently satisfied, she nudged it with her nose.

The baby looked up at its mother, its eyes focusing for the first time in its short life on its mother's face. Delilah nudged the baby again impatiently. Then she began licking it gently, until the foal renewed its efforts to rise. Once again, the foal's front legs stretched forward and its hind legs began scrambling. It stumbled, but its back legs were straight. Slowly, one at a time, the baby straightened out its forelegs, and then brought them to an upright position.

"It's standing!" Carole gasped. "Cobalt's foal is standing—and what a beauty!"

The newborn was perhaps three and a half feet tall, almost all of which appeared to be legs. The foal's small body was precariously balanced atop the spindly legs; the only parts of the baby that moved with any assurance were the ears and the tail, all flicking this way and that experimentally. The newborn lifted a foreleg and then put it back down again. The performance was repeated in turn with each leg. It seemed that once the baby was certain each of its legs worked, it was ready to try them out together. While Delilah waited patiently, licking her baby occasionally, the foal got itself turned around and, just the way it was supposed to, it began nuzzling under its mother's belly.

"It's nursing!" Carole gasped. "Can you believe it? That baby is less than fifteen minutes old and it's nursing already."

They watched in silence for a while as the foal nursed and Delilah finished licking her baby's wet coat dry. After just a few minutes, the foal and Delilah both lay down in the straw and, within seconds, both were asleep.

Just then, the girls heard the familiar sound of Judy's truck pulling up to the stable, followed almost immediately by the vet's hurried footsteps.

"How's she doing, Carole? Is she almost ready to deliver?" Judy called ahead.

"Not for at least another year," Carole said.

Stunned, Judy came to a halt by the stall and then put down her bag quietly so as not to disturb the mare and foal. "Oh," she whispered, startled. And then she stood with the girls, circling them with her arms, enjoying the moment. Her eyes sparkled with pleasure. "I've watched scenes like this hundreds of times, you know. It's always the same and it's always absolutely wonderful. Tell me about it," she said excitedly. "Did you actually see the birth?"

"Oh, yes," Stevie piped up. "We watched almost everything, and it was incredible."

Quickly, but including all the details they could recall, the girls filled the vet in on Delilah's delivery. "You were great!" Judy told the girls. "You did everything just right. You didn't need me at all."

"Actually, Judy," Lisa said, "it seemed to me that Delilah did most of the work."

"That's why they call it labor, Lisa. Now, I think I'll check our patients."

While the girls cleaned up the birthing kit and threw away the papers and wrappers from their snack, Judy finished up with Delilah and the foal. By the time they were all done, Max had returned from his trail ride.

"I had no idea she was so close to delivery, Judy," he said, somewhat embarrassed. "I never would have left her unattended."

"It appears to me, Max, that she was very well attended indeed."

"Yes, I think you're right, Judy. These girls did a fine job and I bet Delilah was pleased they were here. How else would she ever have gotten such a nice bow on her tail wrap?"

Stevie, Lisa, and Carole all giggled. Max and Judy joined in the laughter.

"Well, what's our foal, girls, a filly or a colt?"

Carole felt her face flush. "I—I don't know."

"Didn't you look?" Max asked.

"I completely forgot to," Carole said. "I guess I was just too excited that it was a foal at all—you know?"

"I know," Max said, smiling. "Well, Judy, what is it?"

"It's a colt," she told them. "Cobalt sired a son, Carole. Isn't that what you wanted?"

"More than anything in the world," she said.

"You want to name him?" Max asked. "You can have a couple of days to think about it if you'd like."

Carole didn't have to think about that at all. She'd known for months what the son of Cobalt and Delilah would be called. "His name's Samson," she said. Her friends, Max, and Judy all burst into laughter. After all, Samson was a perfect name for Delilah's son.

And Carole knew that Samson would be the finest, strongest, most wonderful horse she'd ever ride.

"DID YOU SEE how his little tail twitched?" Stevie asked excitedly while the three girls shared a soda in the tack room, waiting for Mrs. Lake to come for them.

"Oh, yeah," Lisa said, grinning in recollection. "And he's so cute when he nuzzles Delilah for some milk. It's almost impossible to believe that only an hour ago he wasn't there at all. I mean—well, that was fantastic. And *you* were fantastic, Carole. You really knew what to do!"

Stevie glanced at Carole. The look on her friend's face was total joy. Stevie and Lisa were excited about Delilah's foal, but to Carole, it was really the final success of Cobalt's life. The little black colt was almost a rebirth, for Cobalt and for Carole.

"I may have known some of the things to do, like wrapping her tail and cleaning her up, but I couldn't have done it single-handed. You guys were the ones who did all the work."

"We helped," Lisa said. "But sometimes doing it isn't as important as knowing what has to be done, you know?"

"Let's face it," Stevie said. "We're a team." She raised her hand victoriously. Carole and Lisa both slapped it.

"What is it when three people give 'high fives' at once?" Carole asked. "A high fifteen?"

"Sounds good to me," Stevie said, grinning. "And the really important thing here is that The Saddle Club is working together again. Look what we can accomplish when we team up—a foal! Gee, if that's what *three* of us can do, imagine what would happen if there were more. Why—"

Stevie abruptly stopped talking because she noticed that very suddenly, Lisa was looking decidedly uncomfortable.

"What's up, Lisa? What's the matter?"

Lisa put the soda can on the bench and stared at the floor. Stevie started to feel nervous. It wasn't at all like Lisa to be so awkward.

Finally, Lisa spoke. "I guess I should tell you that there *are* more than three members of The Saddle Club now."

"I just see the three of us," Carole said. "Who else is here?"

"Well, she's not here now," Lisa explained, "but she *is* in the club."

"Who is?" Stevie asked.

"Estelle," Lisa said. "She was voted in as a member at the last meeting."

One look at Carole, and Stevie knew that was news to her as well. "What last meeting?" Stevie asked.

"The one Friday night," Lisa said quickly. "The one *neither* of you came to. That was the meeting that followed the one at TD's that neither of you came to either. At *that* meeting, all the rules I wrote got passed."

"I don't believe this!" Stevie said, stunned. How could one of her best friends be so disloyal? "How could you do something like that without us?"

"Well, you were each so busy doing your thing without *me*—" Lisa began.

"Hold it," Carole said. Both Stevie and Lisa turned to her. Carole was usually the voice of reason. "I have the feeling that we all learned a lesson this afternoon. We'd all totally forgotten that the real purpose of The Saddle Club is to help each other. I mean, that's the way we started and that's the way it's got to be. There's no way I could have helped Delilah by myself. I *needed* the two of you. Over the last couple of weeks, we've all been so busy worrying about our own projects that we haven't been helping each other at all. So, I guess I'm not really surprised that you passed those rules without us, Lisa, and Stevie shouldn't be either. She's been so busy with Nickel and the gymkhana that, well, like I said, I think we all learned a lesson."

"Thanks for understanding, Carole," Lisa said.

"Wait a second, there," Stevie interrupted. "I can understand that too, but there's still a small problem remaining and her name is Estelle Duval."

"What's the problem?" Lisa said defensively. "Isn't she good enough for you?"

"The problem is that the girl has got no horse sense. She doesn't know the front end from the back or the first thing about riding."

"But she's been riding since she was very little!"

"If that's the case, she hasn't learned much in all those years," Stevie said.

"She has her own horse. She told me he's a white horse named Napoleon."

"Like I said: She hasn't learned much," Stevie repeated.

"What do you mean?" Lisa demanded.

"There's no such thing as a white horse, Lisa," Carole explained. Lisa stared at her, confused. "See, all white horses are actually gray. Most of them start out dark-colored and just turn white with age. It's actually a sign of a real beginner when they call horses white."

"But she's not a beginner. For goodness sake, she even told me something that happened when she was about six!"

"What happened?" Stevie asked.

"Well, she was standing up in the saddle, trying to get her balance and tugging at her horse's mane. The mare got angry and kicked at her."

"Lisa," Carole began, "horses don't have any feeling in their manes. There are no nerves there at all. There's no way that would make a horse 'angry.' Besides that, horses just plain don't try to kick their riders when they're on their backs. A lot of times they'll buck, sometimes they'll try to nip a rider with their teeth, every once in a while they'll rear, or just plain run away, but they only kick at something or someone on the ground."

"You mean it couldn't happen that way?" Lisa asked.

"That's what I mean."

"Well, maybe she forgot. After all, she was pretty little, but she wasn't so young when she was taking care of Napoleon when he was sick and he threw up on her. That just happened last year!"

Stevie's heart went out to Lisa. It was hard to believe anybody could have been taken in by these stories, and because Lisa was such a trusting person it seemed especially cruel of Estelle. "She's told you another tall tale," Stevie began.

"How do you know?" Lisa asked.

"Because horses don't throw up. I mean, they can't. Physically, they don't work that way. It's one of the reasons a colicky horse is such a problem. They'd be better off sometimes if they could just get rid of what's causing the stomachache, but they can't."

"Why would Estelle say something that wasn't true? She doesn't have any reason to lie to me. After all, she's the one with the glamorous life, the fancy schools and friends, the country estate. . . ."

"Oh, you think so?" Stevie asked.

"I don't think we've been fair to Lisa," Carole said to Stevie. "Both you and I knew right away that she was a phony—at least when it came to horses—because she couldn't ride very well. We assumed that Lisa would recognize that, too."

"Isn't all the trouble she's had riding just because of adjusting to American horses?" Lisa asked, defending herself.

"We joke about it, but Max is really right that horses don't speak English, you know," Carole said. "There's no difference among good riders throughout the world."

"How could I know that?" Lisa asked.

"Of course you couldn't," Carole consoled her. "You're such a good natural rider that we sometimes forget what you *don't* know. That's kind of our fault. What you have, though, is really much more important than a lot of facts—you have a real feeling for horses and for riding. Stevie said it a few minutes ago. It's horse sense. You've got it. Estelle doesn't."

"Thanks," Lisa said. "I appreciate your vote of confidence, but the fact remains that as of Friday night, Estelle Duval is a member of The Saddle Club."

"Not for long," Stevie said. "Or else I'm not."

They were just words that Stevie had spoken, but they felt like a bomb to Lisa. As sure as she'd ever known anything, she knew that Stevie meant them. She looked to Carole for consolation, but there wasn't any there.

"Lisa, I think it's up to you," Carole said. Lisa didn't know what to say then. She only knew how she felt and it was bad. She was going to have to choose between her friends and her mistake. What good was horse sense if you could still get into messes like that?

Carole started to speak. Lisa thought maybe she had a suggestion, but before she really got going, Stevie's parents and all three of her brothers bounded into the tack room.

"Can I see the baby?" asked her younger brother, Michael. "Please?"

Stevie was actually happy to see them all. She knew that what she'd said about The Saddle Club was upsetting both her friends, so a change of subject right then was a good idea. But just because she didn't want to talk about her announcement anymore didn't mean she wasn't serious about it. She didn't want any part of Estelle Duval. Ever.

"Come on, guys, let's introduce my family to Samson." She linked arms with Carole and Lisa and led everybody on tiptoe to see the newborn.

When the girls had left Samson only a half hour before, he'd been sleeping soundly. Now, just a short time later, he was back up on his feet, walking around on his spindly legs and checking out his surroundings.

Michael climbed up on the slats of the stall's wall to see better. Samson glanced up at him, his soft brown eyes decidedly curious.

"Wow!" said Michael.

Stevie couldn't have said it better.

12

LISA KNEW SHE ought to feel really excited, sharing in the fun of Samson's birth, but when the sun woke her up the next morning, all she actually felt was dread. Stevie and Carole had made their positions clear. It was Estelle or them.

At first, she thought maybe she could bring her friends around, but when she'd tried to raise the subject once again on the trip home it became clear that Carole and Stevie were totally together. Lisa had made a mistake, a bad one, and she was going to have to correct it.

Correcting mistakes was sometimes impossible and never any fun. Lisa pulled the pillow over her head to shut out the sunlight. Maybe morning would go away.

"Lisa! Breakfast is on the table, dear," her mother called up. "I made you some oatmeal. . . ."

And now she had *that* to contend with, too!

By the time she arrived at the stable, she found that she didn't feel any better at all. She didn't much want to see Carole and Stevie and she certainly didn't want to see Estelle. In fact, she didn't much want to be there at all. Lisa knew that some people would have pretended to be sick, but if she'd done that her mother would have known something was wrong and then she'd have had to answer dozens of questions from *her*.

Lisa was relieved to find that the locker area and the tack room were completely empty. Not surprisingly, everybody was hanging around by the foaling stall, looking at the new baby. Lisa would have joined them, but for three things: Stevie, Carole, and Estelle.

She stowed her lunch in the little refrigerator and lingered in the tack room.

"Aren't you going to see the foal this morning?" Mrs. Reg asked.

"I guess so, in a minute. The whole wide world is there now, aren't they?"

"Yes, they are," Mrs. Reg said, laughing. "Say, while you're waiting, will you give me a hand with something?"

"Sure," Lisa agreed, wondering quickly if maybe, just maybe, Mrs. Reg's chore might take all day.

"I seem to have a whole lot of little pieces of tack and other stable hardware that need to be sorted and stored. Can you do that while I work on the schedule for the three-day event?"

"Oh, I'd be glad to," Lisa told her. She found herself looking at a jumble of metal rings, loops, hooks, bits, and stirrups. She began sorting them into piles of like items. "This is neat stuff," Lisa said, gazing at all the hardware in front of her.

"It's a mishmash of things—harness hooks, rings, double-end snaps, S-hooks, cross-tie chains. All of those are used in the stable, but none of them can be used if we don't know what we've got."

"How do you know what all these things are and what they do?" Lisa asked.

"Oh, you learn, Lisa. After all, you've just started riding. You can't expect yourself to know everything right away."

"That's what *you* think," Lisa said. Just when she wanted to think about it the least, Mrs. Reg had reminded her how little she actually knew about horses.

"You know, there was a boy here once, a new rider . . ."

"Who was that?" Lisa asked, making a chain of S-hooks. Mrs. Reg was famous for her riding stories. This could be fun.

"He was a youngster. He came into the stable knowing almost nothing about horses or riding or anything, but he was very eager to learn. It was okay when he first began. He knew he didn't know anything, so he asked questions all the time and tried to learn as much as he could. After he'd been riding here a few months, though, he got into some trouble."

"How's that?" Lisa asked.

"Well, he started thinking he knew a lot more than he did and he stopped asking questions. One day, he wanted to ride a particular horse, nice little bay gelding we had named Hickory. My husband was watching Hickory, though. He thought he showed signs of lameness. This young rider thought he knew more than my husband and took the horse out anyway— without even asking why he'd been put in a different stall. Within fifteen minutes, the horse was so lame that the rider had to get off him. Took him hours to walk him back to the stable. Vet's bill was something awful, I'll tell you. He had a bowed tendon, and even after he'd healed, he was never as good as he had been."

"But how did that happen? Did the young rider hurt the horse?"

"In a way," Mrs. Reg said. "It turned out that all that had been wrong in the first place was that he had a stone in his shoe. My husband needed a better light to find it and that's why he'd moved him to another stall, intending to check the hoof when he had time. Then, when this young rider took poor old Hickory out on the trail, the horse favored his sore foot. He stumbled, and gave his own leg a good kick, tearing his own tendon."

"You must have been furious," Lisa said.

"Oh, we were," Mrs. Reg said. "It's awful when things go wrong with a horse."

"I bet you never let that rider back here, did you?"

"We couldn't do that," Mrs. Reg said.

"Why not?"

"It was our own son, Max, who did it!"

"Max? My teacher?"

"The very one," Mrs. Reg said. "Of course, he's learned a lot since then—and he's never stopped asking questions, either. Once he got an idea of how much he *didn't* know, and understood that it was all right not to know, things went much smoother for him."

"I think you're trying to tell me something, Mrs. Reg," Lisa said.

"You almost finished with the sorting?" Mrs. Reg asked.

"Just about."

"Max used to like to play with this stable hardware when he was a boy. He'd make chains just like the one you made with the S-hooks, and he'd put a dozen rings on a crop and ride around trying to keep them all on."

"He was a little devil, wasn't he?" Lisa asked.

Mrs. Reg chuckled. "It's almost class time now, Lisa. You'll have to saddle up. Thanks for your help."

Lisa put the sorted hardware into buckets and then stood up to leave. She looked slyly at Mrs. Reg, who was so busy jotting notes on the paper in front of her that she appeared to be unaware of Lisa at all. Lisa doubted that. In fact, Lisa strongly suspected that Mrs. Reg never missed anything at all. Not a thing.

A few minutes later, Lisa was in Pepper's stall, lifting his saddle on. She heard Estelle next to her, working with Patch. Max had let her switch from Nero to another horse. Estelle was having a terrible time with the bridle. She spoke rapidly to the horse in French, but it wasn't doing any good. Estelle was clearly getting angrier and angrier.

As soon as Lisa finished smoothing a wrinkle in the saddle pad and tightening Pepper's girth, she went to Estelle's aid—Patch's, really. Patch was happily walking backward in circles while Estelle chased him with the bridle in her hands. She'd never get the tack on that way.

"Here, Estelle, I'll give you a hand," Lisa offered.

"Oh, this dumb horse. He just wants to give me trouble."

"No, I think he's having too much fun with the game. You can't let a horse get away with that kind of stuff, you know. Here, you hold him. I'll put the bridle on. If he keeps backing up, you should just cross-tie him. Otherwise, you're just teaching him bad habits."

"This horse already knows bad habits. I never had such trouble with horses before I came here."

"Perhaps that's because you never rode before," Lisa said.

"*Moi?*" Estelle asked. "But I have been riding since I was a little girl—from before my seventh birthday."

Something about the mention of her seventh birthday rang a bell to Lisa. She began remembering two other stories Estelle had told her, and they didn't fit at all.

"Was that the seventh birthday you spent in the hospital, or the seventh birthday when you got Napoleon and rode him for hours?"

"I don't know what you mean," Estelle said.

"Estelle, what I mean is that you've been lying to me. You really don't know the first thing about horses. You've hardly ever ridden before and you didn't want to admit it, so you made up stories. You probably made up all the other stories about yourself, too. Your princess friend and your four languages, and your country estate. As a matter of fact, considering the lies I know you've told me, I've begun to suspect that you've never told me the truth at all, have you?"

Estelle looked so shocked that Lisa knew that finally she had found the absolute truth.

"You know, there's nothing wrong with being a beginner at riding. I'm a beginner myself. Sometimes I hate how much I don't know, but I'm not ashamed of it. You can't learn if you can't admit what you don't know."

"I have studied riding with the finest instructors in Europe!" Estelle proclaimed. "But riding here is very different, and not nearly as good."

"If you want to be that way, Estelle, okay," Lisa said. "But I know—"

"What do you know? You and your silly friends and your club! I don't want to be in your club and I don't want to wear that cheap pin! Here, take it back!"

Estelle fumbled in the pocket of her breeches and pulled out the silver horse head. Glaring at Lisa, she threw it into the soiled bedding in Patch's stall. Carefully, Lisa handed Patch's reins to Estelle. She turned and retrieved the pin from the straw. She wiped it off, opened the clasp, and put it on her blouse. It was just as beautiful to her now as it had been the first time she'd seen it in the jewelry store showcase. She'd wear it with pride.

She turned and walked out of Patch's stall. It was time for class and it was time to get back to her horse crazy friends, Stevie and Carole.

Lisa didn't speak to Estelle again that day. The next time she saw her, in fact, Estelle was carrying all her belongings to the car, where her mother was waiting for her. Just at the moment when she might possibly have been ready to be a beginner—an honest beginner—she was quitting. Lisa certainly wouldn't miss her and neither would her friends. It was just too bad, Lisa thought, that Estelle would never really know how much fun riding could be. That was Estelle's loss, but for now, it was The Saddle Club's gain. Lisa could hardly wait to tell Stevie and Carole.

"THAT'S GOOD NEWS," Stevie agreed as the three of them ate their sandwiches together. They were sitting on the grass by the paddocks, enjoying the fresh breeze. "But here's the bad news . . ."

"What's the matter?" Carole asked. It was unlike Stevie to be serious, but the look on her face said she was just that.

"The bad news is that Mrs. Reg and Max are going to be furious with me when I tell them that I haven't come up with one decent game for the gymkhana."

"But you had such neat ideas," Lisa said. "There's something the matter with them all?"

"None of them works, that's what's the matter. I really want this gymkhana to be new and different, and unless I get on it right away, it's not only not going to be new and different, but it's not going to be—*at all*!"

"Wait a second," Carole stopped her. "Nobody here has ever been in a gymkhana before, except maybe me. It's all new and different to all of us!"

"Don't tell me the one about the eggs," Stevie groaned.

"What's the matter with an egg race?" Lisa asked. "Boy, I bet it's funny if somebody drops an egg and it breaks."

Stevie tilted her head and looked at Lisa. "Think it would be funny?"

"Yeah, I do," Lisa said.

"Me too," Carole told her.

"Okay, I give up. We'll have an egg race. What else?"

"What about Laser Tag?"

"I can't borrow it from the Zieglers, so that's out."

"If we can't play Laser Tag, which, by the way, only two people could play at once anyway, how about shadow tag?" Lisa asked.

"Hey, shadow tag? That would be *great*! But what if it rains?"

"Well, then how about some kind of musical chairs? The riders go around a bunch of chairs and when the music stops, they dismount—you get the idea."

"I like it!" Stevie said.

"You know what makes a neat relay race?" Carole asked. "The one where people put on costumes. Everybody looks so silly."

"My mother has saved all the Halloween costumes each of us ever wore," Stevie said, suddenly very excited. "That would be just great—pirates, ghosts, all that stuff. . . ."

"I was in Mrs. Reg's office today," Lisa said. "She has buckets and buckets of hardware, like S-hooks and rings and things like that. There are zillions of things you can do with that sort of stuff. How about stacking rings on a riding crop, or keeping a chain of S-hooks from breaking up while the horse gallops. You know, two riders could be sort of attached to each other with some sort of chain and have to follow a certain course—"

"That's the old rope race," Stevie said, disappointed.

"Sounds to me like a new and different version of 'the old rope race,'" Carole said.

"It does, at that," Stevie agreed. "Listen, I've got an idea, if you don't mind."

"What's that?" Lisa asked.

"I know we were going to practice our drill exercises today, to music, but do you think we could put that off a day or two and work out the fine points of some of these races? I could really use some help with it."

Carole and Lisa exchanged grins. "What else are friends for?" Carole asked.

"What about Simon Says on horseback?" Lisa asked. "And you know what else might be fun? Like maybe as a finale or something, how about a scavenger hunt? Hey, would a horse be spooked by a bouncing ball? I mean we could have a basketball-dribbling race. Imagine how it would look with the balls bouncing all over the place. I think a blind man's bluff would be dangerous, but how about some kind of, say, Pin the Tail on the Pony? It would have to be a picture of a pony, of course. All this stuff's old hat when the kids are on the ground, but they're really different games on horseback, right?" Lisa was about to go on. She hadn't even gotten to her idea about the tennis ball on the racket, but she noticed that both Stevie and Carole were staring at her. "Is something wrong?" Lisa asked.

"Nothing at all," Stevie said reassuringly. "I just never had any idea that you were so full of ideas for horseback games."

"See what I meant?" Carole asked Stevie. "This girl's got horse sense."

"I think she just likes to have fun," Stevie joked.

"With my friends," Lisa told them. She reached up in the air with her hand. Carole's and Stevie's hands met with hers. "High fifteen!" they said together.

13

"THERE YOU GO!" Carole hollered at Lisa. "You've just about got it!"

"I know *she's* got it, but what about me?" Stevie yelled back. Her question was punctuated by the unmistakable splat of an egg hitting the ground.

"You have to go get another one, Lisa, and give that to Stevie. The important part is handing the spoon over to her while you're both on moving horses."

Lisa turned her pony, Quarter, around and signaled him to go fast. He scampered back to the bowl where spare eggs were stored. She took another, placed it in the spoon, made a U-turn, and sprinted back to the starting line, where Stevie was waiting for her.

"Now slow down—" Carole instructed from the sidelines.

Lisa reined Quarter down to a trot, then, just as Nickel began to pick up speed, Stevie took the spoon from Lisa, smooth as could be—until Nickel jerked to a stop at the far line and the egg rolled out of the spoon and onto the ground. Splat!

"Hey, this is great!" Carole said.

"If you like scrambled eggs," Stevie said, making a wry face.

"Everybody likes scrambled eggs," Lisa said. "And I never had so much fun on a horse as this. It's a great race and everybody's going to love it—except maybe Red if he has to clean the ring afterward."

"We could use hard-boiled eggs," Carole suggested.

"No way! These raw ones are much more fun," Stevie said. "Okay, now we've figured out how this one works; we can't try the costume race until tomorrow. I'll bring our whole costume box then so we can sort out things that are equally hard. I mean, it's not fair to have one team just have to slip on a sheet while another has to put on a whole lot of pirate stuff! We'll just have to see how it goes tomorrow. For now, though, what can we do with all the hardware Lisa borrowed from Mrs. Reg?"

Together, they examined the booty. Within a few minutes, they'd designed a race that involved picking up a double-end snap from one of the pillars on the course and then attaching it to a chain suspended from another pillar. When they tested it, they found it was tricky holding the pony still with one hand and trying to fasten the snap with the other.

"Perfect," Stevie announced. "It's good and devious, but it's not impossible. Just the kind of thing I wanted. Now, what were you suggesting about holding a lot of rings on a riding crop?"

"I think first the rider has to sort of scoop them up from someplace, don't you?" Lisa asked.

"Yeah, but how?" Stevie asked. It took a little longer to solve that problem, because it took a while to figure out how the rings could be scoopable, but eventually they discovered that the rings stood up nicely in a glob of bubble gum, which could be perched atop the chest-high pillar.

"Great, that's another. We've gotten more done in an hour together than I could accomplish in ten days by myself."

"It's too bad you didn't ask us for help earlier," Carole said.

"Well, that's the way Niagara Falls," Stevie said philosophically. "And speaking of Niagara Falls, how about something with water? Like maybe the riders get a cupful of water and have to race to the end with it and pass it off to a teammate—sort of a variation on the egg race, but the water's going to splash out!"

"And the winner is the team that finishes with the most water," Lisa chimed in.

"I like it," Carole said. "Let's give it a trial. I'll get some paper cups."

Fifteen minutes later, all three girls had been completely sloshed with water. Their breeches were wet, the ponies' saddles were wet, and they'd had a wonderful time.

"That was so much fun that I think we'll have to do something else with water," Stevie said.

"Water-gun target shooting?"

"Bingo!" Stevie yelled.

WHEN IT CAME time to leave, the girls reluctantly untacked the ponies. Even Nickel and Quarter seemed sorry to stop for the night.

"Don't worry, guys," Stevie consoled Nickel as she slid his stall door closed. "There's lots more work to do, and lots more fun to have. We'll be back tomorrow, okay?"

"Why are all the ponies named after money?" Lisa asked.

"It's one of those Pine Hollow traditions," Carole explained. "Max names them after 'small change,' because of their small size. Some people think ponies are young horses, but that's not true. They're small horses. These guys," she said, pointing to Nickel, Quarter, and their stablemates, Penny and Tuppence, "are all full grown. Their small size makes them perfect for the kinds of games we've been working on. Even the littlest kids can ride them and they're very agile."

"Speaking of small horses, let's go take a look at Samson," Stevie suggested. The girls stowed the pony tack and then walked softly to Samson and Delilah's stall.

"He's grown already, hasn't he?" Lisa asked.

"Oh, yes. He's already bigger and stronger," Carole said excitedly. "Look how he's sort of frisking around the stall. That's not going to be big enough for him in a few days. Just wait until the two of them get out in the paddock. Judy said they could go outside in a few days. He's going to love it. Delilah will too. Horses were born to be outside. Stalls aren't natural for them. They were invented for people's convenience. On my farm, horses will spend almost all their time in the paddocks—"

"Stop her, Lisa. If she gets going on 'her farm,' we'll *never* get out of here!" Stevie said in mock alarm.

"I know, I do talk a lot, don't I?" Carole asked.

"Only about horses," Lisa said, consolingly.

"Let's go to TD's," Stevie invited her friends. "I think we have some celebrating to do."

"We'll make it a Club meeting, then, won't we?" Lisa suggested.

"Why not?" Stevie agreed. "It's about time we all went to one together," she said, joking at her own expense.

A HALF AN hour later, tired, but happy, the three girls settled into a booth at TD's and ordered some ridiculous concoctions. Stevie asked for a pineapple sundae with marshmallow fluff. Carole slapped her hand over her mouth, pretending to gag.

"You should talk," Stevie teased. "You think I want the hot fudge on pistachio you ordered?"

"I think sundaes are very personal," Lisa interrupted. "And personally, I want hot fudge too." The waitress jotted that down. "On bubble gum crunch."

"I'm not saying a thing," Stevie announced. "Lisa's right. Sundaes *are* very personal, and personally, I don't want what either of you ordered."

"Agreed," Carole said sensibly. "Now, to the first piece of business at this official meeting of The Saddle Club . . ."

"About the rules," Lisa began.

"Yes, about the rules—" Stevie said.

"No, let me talk," Lisa interrupted. Carole and Stevie were quiet. Lisa continued, "I had this idea, see, that if we didn't have rules, and purposes, and dues, that we couldn't be a real club."

"How could—" Stevie started to speak, but Carole's slight frown made her halt.

"But I've been thinking about it," Lisa went on, "and it seems to me that every club should be what all its members want it to be. Rules have a place in the world—we all need them. But we don't need them all the time, and not everything is ruled by rules. Some things are ruled by—"

She stopped because she was looking for the right word. Stevie supplied it. "Horse sense, you mean?"

"Yes, that's exactly what I mean," Lisa said, grinning. "Some people might call it common sense, but in The Saddle Club, it *ought* to be known as horse sense. Okay, so we don't need a lot of new rules. Mostly, we just need the ones we already had, like we have to help each other—the way we've been helping Stevie with making up gymkhana races."

"And members have to be horse crazy," Carole added.

"And they have to have horse sense," Stevie continued.

"And that's it," Carole finished.

"Not quite," Lisa said. "There's one thing I did that I didn't even put in the rules, but I think we should use it anyway." Lisa could feel her friends shift nervously. They really didn't want any rules at all. Their friendship and love of horses were enough.

"What's that?" Stevie asked hesitantly.

"Well, real clubs—and I know now that this is a *real* club—usually have symbols like shirts and ties and banners, stuff like that. The Saddle Club now has an official Club pin—and this is it."

She pointed to the shiny horse-head pin on her blouse.

"Hey, that's neat," Stevie said. "I didn't notice it before, but I like it."

"Me too," Carole added. "Where did you get it? Can we buy them too?"

"You don't have to," Lisa said, feeling terribly excited now that her nice secret was going to be shared. "I have one for each of you, too. Here they are." Proudly, she handed the identical pins to her friends. Proudly, they pinned them on their blouses just as Lisa had.

"That's cool," Stevie said. "I never would have thought of something like that, but I like it a lot."

"Actually," Lisa confessed, "I bought four of them. So now we have a spare pin, just in case it should ever happen that we find a person who deserves it."

"I've seen lots of horse pins, but this is the prettiest," Carole told Lisa. "Only you would think of something neat like this, Lisa. You've got a special kind of, oh, I don't know—"

"Horse sense?" Lisa suggested.

"That's exactly right," Carole said. "Dare I call it *le mot juste?*"

For a moment, just a moment, Lisa held her breath. Was Carole teasing her about Estelle? Yes, she was, Lisa decided, and moreover, she deserved it! Her solemn face broke into a grin and then she burst into giggles. Stevie and Carole joined in. They were still laughing when their sundaes arrived.

ABOUT THE AUTHOR

BONNIE BRYANT is the author of more than forty books for young readers, including novelizations of movie hits such as *Teenage Mutant Ninja Turtles* and *Honey, I Shrunk the Kids*, written under her married name, B. B. Hiller.

Ms. Bryant began writing The Saddle Club in 1986. Although she had done some riding before that, she intensified her studies then and found herself learning right along with her characters Stevie, Carole, and Lisa. She claims that they are all much better riders than she is.

Ms. Bryant was born and raised in New York City. Her husband and sometime coauthor, Neil Hiller, died in 1989. She lives in Greenwich Village with her two sons.

THE SADDLE CLUB

A blue-ribbon series by Bonnie Bryant

Stevie, Carole and Lisa are all very different, but they *love* horses! The three girls are best friends at Pine Hollow Stables, where they ride and care for all kinds of horses. Come to Pine Hollow and get ready for all the fun and adventure that comes with being 13!